*A*
*Harlequin*
*Romance*

# SURGEON AT WITTERINGHAM

# SURGEON AT WITTERINGHAM

### (Original title: *Take My Hand*)

*by*

## HILDA NICKSON

**HARLEQUIN BOOKS**

**Winnipeg • Canada    New York • New York**

# SURGEON AT WITTERINGHAM

First published in 1965 by Mills & Boon Limited,
50 Grafton Way, Fitzroy Square, London, England,
under the title *Take My Hand*.

Harlequin Canadian edition published February, 1966
Harlequin U.S. edition published May, 1971

Standard Book Number: 373-52986-4.

Printed in Canada

# CHAPTER ONE

NETTA parked her small car to one side of the new Casualty and Emergency Centre, and with a thrill of pride, pocketed her ignition key.

It was good to be alive, and she felt on top of the world. With a light, springy step she walked towards the side door nearest the theatre, her outdoor uniform cap set at a jaunty angle matching her mood.

Only a few short weeks ago, she had been appointed Theatre Sister of the Centre—the culmination of all her hard work and study. And on the strength of her rise in salary, plus what she had managed to save, she had bought her little car, something she had always wanted. Life had never been so good.

She glanced towards the covered way where a couple of ambulances were parked, and the tall, familiar figure of Jerry Somers appeared.

Ah, Jerry, bless his heart, she said to herself affectionately, and changed direction to walk towards him. She and Jerry had been friends for years, since he had been a student, and she a nurse in training. Now he was one of the new surgical registrars, and though appearing casual, was good at his job.

He stood and waited for her to reach him, both hands in his trouser pockets, his white coat wide open, and a broad grin on his face.

"Hello, beautiful. You look in the pink of condition this morning."

"Hello, Jerry. Had a busy night?"

He nodded. "Pretty fair. I'm off to get some shut-eye now. What about tonight? Shall I see you at the Cheshire Cheese?"

"Yes, all right. About seven?"

"I guess so. Look as good as you do this morning and I'm liable to pop the question—put you out of your supense."

Her lips twitched. "What question?" she asked innocently.

But Iris Leighton, Reception Room Sister, came round the corner with Elva Elliott, Sister of Plaster Room.

"Break it up, you two," Elva said good-humoredly. "Time you were on the Job, Netta."

Netta laughed and fell into step with them as they entered the building.

"'Bye, Jerry," she called over her shoulder. "See you——"

"Thank heaven he's not on day duty at the moment," muttered Iris. "I can't stand him at any price."

"Oh, don't be mean, Iris," Elva put in swiftly. "Jerry's all right. In fact he's damned good. Isn't he, Netta?"

Netta nodded. "I think so. But then I'm prejudiced, I suppose."

Iris Leighton's remark had aroused no annoyance in her. Nothing, at the moment, could take away her feeling of well being. And Iris was always carping about something—or somebody.

"Hm! I'll say you are!" Iris grunted, with an oblique glance at Netta from her chilly blue eyes. "But give me an M.O. or surgeon with some dignity like——" She broke off.

"Like Roger Henderson?" finished Elva.

Iris did not answer, but turned into Reception, leaving Elva and Netta to continue to their own departments.

"You know, I think our Iris is really keen on Roger. I could see the beginning of just a weeny bit of color on either cheek."

"Poor Iris!"

"Heavens, you *are* in an expansive mood these days, aren't you? She doesn't need your sympathy, believe me. It's Roger Henderson—or any other man she sets her sights on—that you should feel sorry for."

"Oh, really, Elva, Iris isn't all that bad," said Netta mildly.

"Isn't she? Come down from the clouds, old girl. We've known her long enough. She can be pretty ruthless when she likes—and when there's something she wants."

Netta smiled. "Well, anyway, our senior surgical officer is well able to take care of himself, I'm sure."

The two parted then, Elva to her plaster room and Netta to her threatre, Netta's mind still dwelling for a minute or two on Roger Henderson.

As Iris had said, he was dignified. He was also a good surgeon. One of the best. Netta had worked with him in General Theatre over at the hospital which was in the same grounds as the Emergency and Casualty Centre. He had been at the Witteringham General for six months now, and was still something of an enigma. But Netta liked him, and from time to time wondered about him. He was quiet, extremely courteous, but Netta somehow had the feeling that beneath his veneer of soberness and dignity there was something explosive. Some great strength. A slumbering giant of a man.

She gave a little self-conscious smile at the way her thoughts were wandering. Thank goodness all men were not so mysterious. There was something to be said for a normal uncomplicated person like Jerry.

But with the opening of the new Centre she now came into daily contact with Roger Henderson. He was chief of the Centre and its medical, surgical and nursing staff were getting to be a special, close-knit community.

There was Hugh Raven, anaesthetist and medical officer. Stephen Monro, orthopaedic surgeon, and the two casualty officers, Joe Hemsley and Bob Griffiths, as well as Jerry. Sister Jones—known to everyone as Bobby Jones—who had been the old Casualty Sister, was now the departmental Sister-in-Charge. These, along with three other Sisters besides Elva, Iris and Netta and a complement of staff and student nurses, maintained a twenty-four-hour service. In addition, of course, there were the various visiting consultants.

The Centre was typical of similar ones now springing up in many of the large cities and towns throughout the country. It had its own X-ray department with the main equipment suspended from the ceiling so that patients could be simply wheeled straight underneath instead of having to be lifted from stretcher to equipment as before. To one side of the X-ray department there was a Recovery area, and at the other, Resuscitation, both fitted with piped oxygen and suction, and a special type of sphygmomanometer. The trolleys, too, were of a special design. They had radio-translucent bases, attachments for intravenous transfusion apparatus, and a shelf underneath for patients' clothes, as well as detachable cot sides. And in the plaster room there was an up-to-the-minute hydraulic table with easily manipulated controls for positioning.

As to Netta's own department, this was a fully equipped operating theatre. And it was always busy. Here there were no set operation lists as in an ordinary theatre. Anything could happen at any moment, and Netta took a pride in being always prepared.

One of the most important things—indeed, *the* most important—was in maintaining her pre-package system. Packs of instruments, complete for specific operations, dressing packs, gown and glove packs were always sterile and clearly labelled. With regard to some of the operation packs, it was almost a case of 'one on, one in the wash and one in the kit-bag'. There was no time for the frantic boiling-up of instruments between one operation and the next. If one laparotomy set was in use, there was always another ready and waiting in the autoclave.

The most important of the instrument packs because they were in the most frequent use were, of course, those required for traumatic surgery. The autoclave was never without a thoracotomy set for penetrating wounds of the chest and abdomen, packs for dealing with wounds like compound fractures, and head injuries. Similarly there were always at least two traceostomy sets, and of course, a number of transfusion sets which included instruments for 'cutting down'.

Life was hectic, but Netta loved it. She thrived on emergencies. She had a good theatre staff and——

She pushed open the swing doors leading to the short theatre corridor, and as she passed the surgeons' changing room Roger Henderson suddenly emerged.

"Good morning, Mr. Henderson," Netta said cheerfully, adding a smile for good measure.

None of the staff of the Centre stood on ceremony. Many of the senior nursing staff, and the doctors and surgeons, were on first-name terms. But the only condescension the surgical chief had made was a gruff: 'You can cut out the "sir", Sister', one Sunday afternoon at the termination of a particularly serious emergency operation.

Now he halted momentarily and gave her an unsmiling stare. Netta felt she'd love to shake his dignity, break down his aloofness. His habitual gravity appeared to her as amusing this wonderful morning on which she felt so on top of the world.

11

Her lips twitched a little and she looked up at him —he was tall above average, and she a five foot three—and her eyebrows raised slightly.

"Is anything *wrong*, Mr. Henderson?"

His gaze flickered and he gave her a look of mild surprise, then straightened his hunched shoulders.

"Good morning, Sister. No, there's nothing wrong. Another accident case, that's all."

He strode off, and with an inward, "Ah, well——" Netta went through the nursing staff's changing room to the theatre. The familiar mopping-up business was going on. Theatre was all but ready for action again, and through into the sluice two night nurses were wiping down plastic sheeting, hanging up gloves to dry and clearing up in general, though with the use of disposable theatre caps, gowns and paper towels this was cut down to a minimum.

The night staff nurse in charge was drying instruments. Netta said good morning.

"Had a busy night? Must have been something big just now. I've seen Mr. Henderson—and Jerry Somers. But he didn't say anything."

Nurse Goodall smiled absently. "Well, you know what Jerry is, Sister. Easy come, easy go. There's been a smash-up on the M.I., somewhere around six a.m. It appears they suddenly ran into mist. We got the lot, from cuts and bruises to fractured ribs and internal injuries."

Netta glanced around the sluice. "Yes. Well, you've done your whack. Away you go now. The day nurses can finish off. There isn't much more to do, anyway, by the look of things." She glanced at the number of instruments which had been used. "Looks like two lots there."

The staff nurse nodded. "Mr. Henderson had to do two incisions."

The night staff had no sooner gone than Sister Jones came into the theatre.

"Case for you, Rowlands. Appendix. Anaesthetist and surgeon both on their way."

"Right, Sister."

Netta had three staff nurses on day duty in Theatre, Nurses Kelly, Lewis and White. But is was Nurse Kelly's day off. The other two were in the sterilizing room making up packs.

"There's an appendix coming in," she told them. "I'll scrub, and will you, Lewis, come and do the necessary, then scrub for the next. White, you help Lewis with the next and scrub for the third. That'll be roughly our rota for the day."

"Right, Sister."

No further instructions were necessary. The nurses knew what they had to do. A student nurse would attend to the saline bowls, get gown, sterile towel and glove packs from the autoclave and unfasten their outer layers, then stand by to fasten Netta and the surgeons into their gowns. Staff Nurse Lewis would get the instrument packs and lay them out on the trolleys in the operating theatre. Then she would help the anaesthetist.

Netta began to scrub, and soon she was joined by the anaesthetist, Hugh Raven.

"Hi, Netta," he greeted her. "And how's the world using you this bright morning?"

"Fine, Hugh. Just fine. Never felt better in my life."

He glanced at her as he scrubbed his hands. "You've never looked better, either, as a matter of fact." He grinned. "Jerry got around to proposing at last?"

She laughed. This was a standing joke among those who had known Jerry and herself for some time, and she did not mind in the least.

"That'll be the day!"

"Sure will. And if he doesn't hurry up, somebody will be beating him to it."

She rinsed her hands in a solution of chlorhexidine and extracted a sterile towel from the pack. Her lips curved in good-natured amusement.

"Such as who? Don't tell me you've got designs on me yourself."

Having dried her hands she dropped the towel into a pail and strode over to the gown pack.

"Why not?" answered Hugh. "The way you look this morning, you'd better watch out."

She pulled her gown over her arms and held out the tapes for the nurse to tie her into it.

"I know one person I'm safe from, anyway."

"Who's that?"

Hugh's question came quick as a flash, and Netta wished she had not made that last remark. Why had she? Why was it that all at once, Roger Henderson should keep coming into her mind? It didn't make sense. But she couldn't mention his name to Hugh Raven, particularly when one of the student nurses was standing there.

"Ah, that would be telling," she answered him, as if to tease him.

She drew on her sterile gloves and went into Theatre proper to prepare needles and sutures and to lay out the instruments. Noises off indicated that the patients had been wheeled into the anaesthetic room. Then Hugh went through, pushing his way backwards through the swing doors, his hands wrapped in a paper sterile towel. A moment later she heard the voices of the surgeons in the scrub room.

She frowned a little. One of them sounded like Roger Henderson. She supposed, with Jerry being on night duty, Mr. Henderson had felt he had to take this case himself. But he would barely have had time for breakfast between the accident case and this emergency, she reflected.

But she put her mind to her work. In a few minutes from now, the patient would be ready.

An emergency appendicectomy was often accompanied by peritonitis due to rupture of the appendix. Accordingly, Netta was always prepared. Each appendicectomy pack contained a corrugated rubber drain and safety pin, as well as a sterile specimen jar in case one was needed. And Nurse Lewis, without being prompted, would have everything ready for the giving of an intravenous saline during the operation.

Now the patient was wheeled in and put into position on the table. His skin had already been prepared in Resuscitation. Netta unfolded the operation sheet carefully and placed it over the patient, arranging the cut-out window over the abdominal area. Then she clipped sterile towels in place.

"Thank you, Sister."

No matter what the emergency Roger Henderson was always courteous. But then so was Jerry, in his way. It was either, 'Good show, honey', or 'Thanks, beautiful'.

"Plasma?" asked Hugh.

Roger nodded. Nurse Lewis wheeled a trolley forward, and between them, she and Hugh set up the intravenous while still continuing the anaesthesia.

Roger made a tranverse incision. "We're likely to find a pretty bad case here," he said. "The man's been in pain for three days now. He has his own grocery business out at Sutton, and of course, didn't want to give in. He's only a young man—not yet thirty. Young to have his own business, that is."

"But old for appendicitis," added Hugh.

"Yes."

"Has he a wife?"

"He has, but I got the impression that she's not much help in the business."

Hugh grunted. "Well, maybe this'll learn her."

"Maybe."

Netta continued to pass the required instruments. At the other side of the table to Roger, Joe Griffiths took care of Spencer Well's and dabbed with swabs.

Then: "Suction, Sister."

This was already connected up. Netta handed the sterile end to him and nodded to the student nurse who was already standing by to switch on at the main.

"Rupture here all right. Got a specimen jar handy, Sister?"

"No wonder the man has had so much pain," Roger murmured.

Netta gave him a swift glance. She had never noticed before how sympathetic he could be. Iris Leighton had got something, after all. He was certainly a man to be admired. But not just for his dignity.

"What's the patient's name, sir?" she asked.

For a minute he did not answer. She wondered whether he had heard her. Then he said, without taking his eyes from his work:

"I'm glad you asked that, Sister. It's so easy to forget that, on the operating table, there lies a person, not just a case. His name is Tony. Tony Kilner."

A tiny frown appeared on Netta's brow. Somehow, she felt there was a veiled criticism in his words. She had *never* thought of the patients as merely cases. In an emergency theatre such as this, one could not hope to get to know them as people, of course. And there *were* times when they were so quick in and out one did not even get to know a patient's name. Still, there was no time, either, to be unduly sensitive in this theatre. So she merely said:

"Thank you, sir."

He held out his hand for the drainage and said coolly, "I seem to remember asking you to drop the 'sir', Sister."

"I'm sorry, s—Mr. Henderson."

What on earth was the matter with him this morning? Was he just tired or——

"You don't have to apologize, Sister," he went on smoothly. "It's up to you entirely."

She felt faintly humiliated, but an anger against him began to rise up inside her, an anger that he had introduced into this wonderful morning a note of discord. And to think she had even been concerned as to whether or not he had had breakfast! The fact that he had given his gracious permission for her to stop calling him 'sir' did not guarantee or establish a more friendly relationship overnight—if indeed that was what he wanted. She had not called him that deliberately. She had simply forgotten. After all, if people insisted on standing on their dignity, then——

With an effort she stemmed the flow of her thoughts. It would do no good to rant on like this. She would just have to try to remember, that was all. But she must not let him rob her of the wonderful feeling of well-being she had.

The operation had reached the stage of skin sutures when Roger Henderson's combination of lights flashed on.

"Shall I take a message—Mr. Henderson?" Netta asked.

"No, I'll go," he answered brusquely. "Finish off here, will you, Joe?"

"Yes, Chief."

Joe moved round to the right side of the table, and Roger peeled off his gown and gloves. There was a short silence after the surgeon had gone. Joe carried on with the suturing and Hugh fiddled with his anaesthetic machine, then stood up.

"He'll be all right now. Think I'll go and get me a coffee before somebody starts hounding me."

"If the chief was wanted, maybe you will be, too, any minute now," said Joe.

"Not in a very good mood this morning, is he?" murmured Hugh.

"The chief? He was up at crack of dawn. That pile-up on the M.1."

"He's not the only one. I, too, was up at the crack of dawn," Hugh said earnestly. "You can't have an operation without an anaesthetist. Or did you know that?"

"To tell you the truth—no, I didn't," retaliated Joe.

"Well, you know now. No, there's something else biting our Roger, and I think I know what it is."

Netta glanced at him swiftly. "And what's that?" she murmured.

"Ah, that would be telling, wouldn't it?" he grinned, flinging her own words back at her.

Much of this chatter would go over the heads of the nurses hovering around, Netta knew that. She remembered her own training days and the muttered snatches of conversation among the seniors around the operating table. Non-scrubbed nurses simply had to be a safe distance in case of contaminating them. In spite of the many changes which had taken place in hospital life, the Sisters, doctors and surgeons still tended to be in a sort of charmed circle. Little bits of conversation, though intelligible to those around the table, often did not make sense to the nurses, fortunately.

Hugh went to get his coffee—on brew every morning in the surgeons' changing room, and the skin sutures now finished, the patient was wheeled into Recovery, and Joe went for his coffee, too.

Netta's nurses were well trained. Within minutes the floor, table and other fittings had been wiped over with disinfectant. Within minutes, too, Roger Henderson was back again.

"Strangulated hernia, Sister. Just as soon as you can be ready. Pre-medication is being given now."

"Are you doing it, Mr. Henderson?" she queried.

"Yes. Why do you ask?"

"Only that this is your third op in succession. Won't you at least go and get some coffee? It's freshly made."

His eyes opened wide and he looked at her suspiciously. But he said in a quiet voice:

"Thanks, Sister. I'll do that."

It was Nurse Lewis's turn to act as instrument nurse. Nurse White attended to anaesthetics and set the intravenous trolley. Thanks to Netta's prepackaging system everything was ready in next to no time, and during the operation she herself washed, dried and re-autoclaved the instruments used for the appendicectomy, also kept an eye on what was happening in the operating theatre. She found this change-over of occupation worked very well indeed.

Roger Henderson seemed to be tireless. By the time the strangulated hernia was finished Netta was lost in admiration for him.

"He must have a constitution like a horse," Hugh grumbled as he wheeled his anaesthetic machine out.

Netta glanced at him curiously. "Is that envy or admiration?" she queried, holding open the door for him.

"It's neither. I've nothing to envy him for— have I? And I don't particularly admire him."

"He's a good surgeon."

"So what? Is he the only one who's good at his job?"

"No-o."

19

"I wouldn't have thought you'd hold any brief for him, anyway, after his churlishness earlier on."

"I don't know that I am holding a brief for him," she protested. "But you have to give people their due."

He gave a grunt of derision. "Some get more than their due. It creases me, it really does. I've been in various hospitals in my time, and no matter what sort of hound the S.S.O. is, there are always two or three—or even more—of the nurses ready to fall in love with him at the drop of a theatre cap, while the poor old M.O. can be as nice and helpful, as decent as it's possible for a fellow to be, but he still can't hold a candle to the great and mighty surgeon."

Netta couldn't help smiling. "Hugh, that's non-sense."

"Is it? But don't get the wrong idea, Sister dear. As far as I'm concerned personally, I don't give a damn. I'm just making an observation," he said lightly.

"All right. Point taken. Mind you, I think anaesthetists are pretty wonderful people, myself."

He grinned. "You do? Then how about a date some time? Tonight, perhaps."

She moved towards the door. "Sorry, Hugh. No can do tonight. Seeing Jerry."

"There you are, you see! Another surgeon. I tell you, the poor M.O. doesn't stand a chance, even if he is an anaesthetist as well."

She laughed. Hugh was only joking, of course. "Diddums", she teased. "Seriously, though, Jerry and I have been friends for years, and it's nothing to do with his being a surgeon. In any case——"
But she left the rest unsaid. She didn't want to add that she wasn't in love with Jerry.

Hugh came towards her, eyeing her question-ingly. "I wouldn't be breaking anything up between you two, then, if I took you out one evening? If you'd come, that is."

"Ask me again some other time, Hugh," she said, flashing him a smile. "I must go now."

She pushed her way out of the swing doors again. There was very little time for dallying in any part of the Centre, and it was getting on for twelve o'clock. Time to send some of the nurses to first lunch.

Apart from the manipulation of a fracture, done by Stephen Monro, the orthopaedic surgeon, there was very little in Theatre during the afternoon except for minor surgery. As this was handled by either Joe or Bob, Netta did not see Roger Henderson again that day. Hugh was busy elsewhere, too, though she did catch a glimpse of him once in the Resuscitation area. She thought of them both, in a vague sort of way, and in particular about what Hugh had said. He was right, really. In hospital, there did seem to be a sort of glamour surrounding the surgeons. And the more dignified and aloof they were, the more some nurses and Sisters appeared to like them. She smiled to herself. She wasn't one of them, at any rate. Mr. Henderson could be annoying at times, but she certainly wasn't ready to fall in love with him at the drop of a hat, theatre or otherwise.

At five o'clock she handed Theatre over to Nurse Lewis and went off duty. She remembered that Elva was off for the evening, too, and popped her head round the plaster room door.

"Like a lift, Elva?"

"You bet! Shan't be a minute. Just got to wash my hands. Had a busy day?"

"Not bad. The morning was the worst."

They talked the usual shop-talk, then left by the front entrance.

"Wish I could afford a car," Elva sighed, as they walked towards Netta's. "I must have been spend-

21

ing my money instead of saving it, I suppose. I've got *some,* but not enough even for a deposit. And it's no good buying a cheap one. It would cost the earth in repairs. Apart from that, I'd be scared stiff of the thing breaking down miles away from anywhere."

"Do you know, that possibility never even occurred to me," Netta said, opening both doors. "But this isn't a new one. You can get very good second-hand cars."

But Elva went on to say that she doubted, anyway, whether she'd have the nerve to learn to drive.

"When you see some of the human wrecks we get in the Centre, it makes you think twice."

Elva shuddered, and though Netta agreed with her, she couldn't help laughing at Elva's varied reasons for not having a car of her own while professing she'd like one.

"But that reminds me," Elva said, though how one thing reminded her of another Netta couldn't quite see. "I meant to ask you before. You remember asking me if I'd like to share your flat with you some time ago?"

"Yes. You'd already promised to share one with a cousin or something."

"That's right. Well, she's got another job—down London way somewhere. And as I'm getting fed up with my landlady——"

"Come and share with me, by all means," Netta said quickly. "I'll be glad to have you. It's a bit on the expensive side for me now that I've got the car, but Mrs. Morney is such a sweetie, I didn't want to leave. There's that lovely big room and kitchen upstairs, as you know, and she's always telling me that if I want to have a friend in for the evening I can use the sitting room downstairs. By that, of course, she means "gentlemen friends." And, as a matter of fact, Jerry has been in a few times. She's a little bit old-fashioned, and doesn't think it's right to have a lone male up in the bed-sitting room."

"Well, of course, it's her house——"

"Exactly. And she considers me her guest rather than her tenant. She does all kinds of little things for me. Shopping, cooking and so on. I'm really very fond of her."

"When can I move in, then? You'll have to ask her first, I suppose?"

"A mere formality, I'm sure. I'll speak to her tonight as soon as I get in."

Netta made a slight detour so that she could drop Elva off at the house where she lived, then went on to her own place.

As she had told Elva the bed-sitting room she rented was really intended for two. It was a large room on the first floor of a Victorian family house nicely furnished with a comfortable lounge suite and two divan beds and a rich thick-pile Indian carpet on the floor. What was once its attached dressing-room made a small kitchen. She shared a bathroom with Mrs. Morney.

Netta made herself some tea, then changed to go out to meet Jerry.

# CHAPTER TWO

THE Cheshire Cheese was a popular rendezvous with a good many of the hospital staff, doctors and nurses alike. It was a friendly place, its waiters, waitresses and bar attendants more like old friends than men and women merely doing a job of work. The low tables and comfortable, chintz-covered chairs of the Club Room contributed to the 'at home' atmosphere, and one could always be sure of seeing a familiar face, always get a snack with one's drink, and in the Grill Room be guaranteed a meal which, though not elaborate, was both enjoyable and satisfying.

Jerry was waiting for Netta in the Club Room. "Hello, beautiful," was his characteristic greeting. "Still feeling on top of the world in spite of your usual gruelling day?"

She laughed and sat down beside him on one of the settees. "Oh, I wouldn't call it gruelling, really, though of course, it's had its moments. Did you sleep well?"

"Like a top. And I shall sleep tonight, too. Dreaming, oh, my darling love, of thee," he added with a grin.

"I'm sure. Who's on tonight, then?"

"Bob. But what will you have to drink?"

"Er—sherry, thanks."

He attracted the attention of one of the waiters and ordered her drink and another for himself.

"I suggest we go into the Grill Room in a minute or two and have something to eat. I don't know about you, but I feel as though my stomach's saying how d'you do to my spine."

"I expect I shall be able to peck a little, too."

She gave him a smile, but all at once he looked serious. Her eyes twinked.

"Surely the pain isn't that bad, Jerry?"

"Eh?" he said blankly.

She laughed. 'You *must* be hungry! I think we'd better go and get that meal before you start nibbling at the chair covers or something."

He looked at her for moment, then grinned. "I'll start on you. You look good enough to eat, anyway."

"Would you like me to go and find some pepper and salt?" she teased.

"Yeah—some mustard too while you're about it. But here comes Len with our drinks."

He had a few words with the waiter and paid him, then said, in between taking a drink:

"How about going for a run somewhere after we've eaten?"

"I've got my own car outside."

"Then you can leave it here and pick it up later, because mine's outside, too. Come on, on your feet, girl."

"You're very masterful this evening, aren't you? Do you mind if I take my sherry with me? Er—sir," she added.

He grinned and stood up, offering her his hand. "On your feet, then."

She gave him her hand a little absently and they made their way into the Grill Room. Calling Jerry sir reminded her of Roger Henderson and this morning's scene in Theatre. But it was of no real importance, and she dismissed the matter from her mind.

Jerry was his usual lively self during their meal. Also later, as he drove his red convertible at a fast, but not dangerous speed along the arterial road out into the country. It was when they stopped in a lay-by for a cigarette that he became silent. He put his arm across her shoulders as he often did, but sat for so long gazing into space, she gave him an amused glance.

"What's on your mind, Jerry? Or have you gone into a coma?"

He laughed and his arm across her shoulders tightened. "It would be more correct to say, *who's* on my mind."

She raised her eyebrows. "Good gracious! Don't tell me you're in love. It's Autumn, not spring. And besides, I thought you said you were going to pop the question to *me*."

She expected him to laugh, but he didn't. He threw his half-finished cigarette out of the window then drew her towards him, took her cigarette from between her fingers and threw that out of the window, too.

"What on earth——' she protested mildly.

But suddenly he covered her mouth with his. For a minute she made no further protest. There was nothing unusual in Jerry kissing her, but to-night there was something different about him.

"Have a heart, Jerry——" she gasped, pushing him away with a half laugh.

He relaxed his hold. "Sorry and all that, Netta. I guess I got—sort of carried away. You look so different tonight, so—well, you know——"

She laughed. "Really, Jerry! You *are* in a mood, aren't you?"

"I guess maybe we both are," he said in an odd voice, then leaned forward and turned the ignition key.

She frowned a little. "No, Jerry," she said, putting out a restraining hand. "Don't just start up like that. I'm sorry if I pushed you away, but—well, you were a bit——"

She broke off, hoping he would know what she was trying to say.

He dropped his hand down again and leaned back and looked at her, his usual grin on his face.

"I told you you were good enough to eat, didn't I?"

"Well, if you're still feeling hungry, perhaps we'd better go back and get something more to eat," she laughed.

A smile still on his face, he put his arm about her shoulders again.

"To tell you the truth, I've got a bet on with some of the fellers. They bet me that I daren't pop the question tonight. I was trying to work up to it."

"Well, I like that!" she said indignantly.

He took hold of one of her ears and pulled her face round to his.

"I had to do something. To save my face, I mean. I thought it was time I made an honest woman of you."

"That's rich. You're making it up, of course."

"It was worth a try, anyway."

He kissed her again, this time with more restraint, and after a minute or so he took out his cigarette case and offered her one.

"Shall I be allowed to finish this one?" she asked mischievously. "You've simmered down?"

For answer he flicked his lighter, and when both their cigarettes were lighted, she rested her head on his shoulder as she often did, and they smoked in peaceful silence. Jerry fondling her ear absently.

Netta sighed contentedly. She really was awfully fond of Jerry. This was a wonderful relationship they had, and she wouldn't want it any other way.

"What's the sigh for?" he asked.

"Oh—I'm just feeling happy, I suppose. Life's pretty good when you think of it. We've got that marvellous centre, everybody works well together, I've got my little car and——"

"And?" he prompted.

She turned her face towards him and smiled, letting her gaze take in his familiar features, his high forehead, rather large nose and generous mouth. Not a handsome face, but a very pleasant and intelligent one.

She touched his nose. "And I've got you," she said, half teasingly.

His eyes widened. "Better watch out," he warned.

She laughed and threw away her cigarette, then touched his cheek fondly.

"You know, Jerry, I think it's wonderful—a friendship like ours. Honestly. Don't you?"

"Sure. Just great. Nobody asking too much, nobody wanting to get married or any of that nonsense——"

"That's exactly what I mean!" She was so happy that he felt the same. Just now when he kissed her, she had been just a little bit afraid that he was becoming serious. "Of course, I suppose we shall both get married some time. But at the moment, our sort of friendship is just fine, isn't it?"

He nodded. "Just fine."

She rested her head on his shoulder again. She could almost fall in love with Jerry. Would they, one day? she wondered. But no. Not after all this time. If they had been going to fall in love with each other, they would have done so years ago. In any case, though she was fond of him—and he of her, she simply could not imagine either of them becoming romantic about each other.

Jerry finished his cigarette, then started up the car again. Driving back to town he began to sing as he often did at the wheel, and Netta joined in, feeling great.

"Would you like to slip into the Cheese before you go home?" he asked as they entered the thirty-mile speed limit. "It's still quite early. We made better time than I realized."

"You mean you wanted to get back before closing time," she teased him.

"Cut out the funny stuff. Are you coming or aren't you?"

"Well, I've left my car there, in any case. Had you forgotten?"

"I had, as a matter of fact. I haven't got used to the idea of you having your own car yet. Well that settles it. You can pop in and have a quick one with me. That landlady of yours won't let you ask me up for a coffee, so——"

"Jerry! I've suddenly remembered something. I must get back to the flat. There's something I want to see Mrs. Morney about, and she goes to bed early."

He glanced at the dashboard clock. "What? At only just turned half past nine? You must be joking."

"No, I'm not. She takes a pile of books to bed with her."

"Lord! I could think of more exciting things to take to bed with me."

"I dare say you could. But Elva Elliot wants to move in with me, and I promised to ask Mrs. Morney about it tonight."

He turned in to the car park of the Cheshire Cheese. "All right, honey. You win. See you around, then. Maybe we'll do a show next time, eh?"

He drew her towards him and kissed her goodnight as he always did, and on a sudden impulse she put her arms around his neck and kissed him in return with a special warmth.

"Hey, what's this?" he asked, gripping her shoulders and eyeing her cautiously.

"Oh—just to show you how much I care and all that," she told him laughing. "Goodnight, Jerry, and God bless."

She reached out for the handle of the door, but he kept his hold on her.

"Ah, now wait a minute. You can't say things like that, then just say goodnight."

"Oh, but I can. Wolf!"

"Wolf? I like that! Chance would be a fine thing."

"Yes, wouldn't it?" she laughed, and broke free of him. She opened the door and got out, saying a last goodnight, and was in her own car before he had left his.

Mrs. Morney was perfectly willing for Elva to move in with Netta, and a few days later Netta and Jerry helped her with her luggage and other bits and pieces.

Jerry looked around the spacious room with surprise. "I say, this is quite something. You could have a marvellous party up here."

"Maybe I will now," Netta said. "Or rather, *we* will."

"And maybe I shall be allowed up here occasionally now that there are two of you. Hitherto—as they say in literary and legal circles—I've been confined to the drawing room on Sundays and the hall on weekdays."

"Think yourself lucky you were allowed over the front doorstep," laughed Netta.

Jerry suggested they should all three go along to the Cheshire Cheese for a drink and a snack, and Netta agreed readily. But Elva wasn't too sure.

"I really ought to stay in and do my unpacking. Besides, two's company and all that. I'm sure you two want to be on your own."

Netta stared at her. "Heavens above, what's got into you? You know perfectly well there is nothing like that about me and Jerry. As for your unpacking, you can do that any old time."

"That's right," Jerry put in. "Come on now, Elva, let's have no nonsense. Netta and I don't fuss about being alone, and in any case, you're never alone at the Cheshire Cheese."

One person who was not an habitué of the place, however, was Roger Henderson. But this evening, as it happened, he *was* there, sitting alone at a small table. Netta was the first to see him, and there was something about him which caught at her heart. He looked so lonely.

"Let's ask him to join us, shall we?" she asked the other two.

"Suppose he doesn't want to?" Elva said doubtfully.

"Oh, but surely—I mean nobody's alone because they want to be. At least, not in a place like this."

"There's no *need* for him to be alone," Jerry pointed out. "No need for any man. He can always ask a woman—and there are plenty at the hospital."

"Maybe he's too shy to ask them," Netta insisted.

This brought laughter of derision from both Elva and Jerry.

"Oh, come off it, Netta."

"Aren't you letting your imagination run away with you?"

"Anyway, how do you know he isn't waiting for somebody?" said Jerry.

"Yes. Maybe Iris Leighton's got him into her clutches at last," Elva said.

"Oh, really, you two!"

But another ten minutes passed by, and still the surgeon sat alone. Netta felt more and more sorry for him.

"I don't care what you say," she declared. "I'm going to ask him. Er—that is, if you've no real objection."

Jerry shook his head in silence, his eyebrows raised, while Elva shrugged and said, "Go ahead."

Netta hesitated for a moment. But as she looked across the room to where he was sitting she caught his eye. She smiled at him, and when he nodded in acknowledgment, she rose and went over to him.

"Good evening, Mr. Henderson."

He rose politely. "Good evening. Would you care to join me, Sister?"

"Well, I——" But she sat down. "As a matter of fact, I came to ask you to join us. Will you? Unless, of course, you're waiting for someone," she added quickly.

31

He looked at her. "That's very kind of you. As a matter of fact, I am waiting for someone, but——"

"Oh." She was rather taken aback. "Oh, then I'd better go. I—I'm sorry——"

But he put out a restraining hand. "No, no, please don't go. Stay and talk to me for a while— if you're sure your two friends won't mind."

She subsided and smiled. "I'm sure they won't. We've—just been helping Sister Elliot to move her things. She's going to share my flat with me. That is, if you can call it a flat. Actually, it's only a bed-sitter, but it's such a large room——"

She broke off, conscious all at once that she was virtually gabbling. This was actually the first time she had had any ordinary conversation with him. She suddenly realized that, too. But really, there was no need for her to carry on as if she were the rawest of student nurses facing an eminent consultant.

"I'm sorry," she said, more normally. "I seem to be hogging the conversation."

"Not at all," he said politely. "It was most interesting. I'm afraid I know very little about any of the staff outside of Theatre, and——"

He broke off, his gaze directed towards the door. Netta turned to see Iris Leighton approaching. From the supercilious glance she gave Netta and the smile she put on for Roger there was no doubt whatever that she was the one for whom he was waiting.

Netta rose to her feet, and with a muttered. "I'll leave you now, then," she went back to Elva and Jerry.

She found them almost convulsed with suppressed laughter.

"Oh, dear," said Jerry. "Poor old Netta. I told you he might be waiting for somebody. That'll learn you not to waste your sympathies."

"Well! So she's done it at last," murmured Elva, wiping her tears of laughter from her eyes, and glancing across at Iris, now sitting at Roger's table. "But who knows? She might be the making of him."

"The making of him?" echoed Netta indignantly. "I'm sure he doesn't need anyone like Iris to do anything for him."

This appeared to amuse Elva greatly, and Jerry looked at Netta with raised brows.

"Hello, hello, why all the indignation? Why this sudden championing of our distinguished surgical chief?"

"And why not?" she countered.

Jerry pursed his lips. Then he turned to Elva, and said, with mock-solemnity: "You know, she's got something there. Why not indeed?"

Elva looked solemnly back at him, and realizing she was having her leg pulled by the two of them Netta burst out laughing.

"Idiots!" she pronounced.

And after looking suitably outraged they laughed, and normal conversation was more or less resumed, though from time to time they still teased her about Roger Henderson.

"But seriously," said Jerry, "he doesn't mix in very much, you know, in the residents' quarters. At least, not with the general rabble. If things get too sort of riotous, he just disappears to his own rooms. In fact, sometimes we don't see him for days except at meal times. I often wonder what he does with himself up there."

"Maybe he's fond of reading."

"In that case he and your landlady should get together," laughed Jerry.

At this point Hugh Raven came in, and Jerry beckoned him over.

"Hello there. Isn't there anyone left at the Centre?"

Hugh pulled up a chair. "There's Joe, and Steve Monro. He's been kept pretty busy." His gaze went round the room and lighted on Roger Henderson. "Heavens above! Look who else is here. Wonders will never cease. And with Iris Leighton."

Jerry nodded. "We nearly had his company, believe it or not. Our dear little Netta here felt sorry for him."

"Oh, why?"

"He looked so lonely. Until Iris came, of course. But then Netta's such a sweetie. She'd feel sorry for anybody, really."

"Well, she's wasting her time on him."

"That's what I told her."

Netta began to feel annoyed. "Look, why are you all so down on him? Just because he's a little different from anyone else, and—and doesn't like being one of a crowd——"

Jerry put his hand swiftly on hers. "Darling, we're only pulling your leg," he said mildly.

But Hugh wasn't teasing. "Why shouldn't he be one of the crowd, anyway? Is he so much better than anyone else?" he demanded.

"He's probably better than some, anyway," Elva put in, much to Netta's relief. "Both in character and at his job. And you've got to allow for some individuality. It wouldn't do for us all to be alike. It would make for a very dull world indeed."

"It would be dull if there were many like him, anyhow," said Hugh.

And at the departure of Roger and Iris the topic of conversation became more general, and Netta was glad, though she didn't think for a moment any of them actually disliked him. Elva had spoken in his favor, Jerry had only been joking, and she felt sure that Hugh did not seriously resent him. It was all no more than idle hospital gossip. Men could be just as guilty of this as women were supposed to be, in spite of what was said to the contrary. She didn't know why it even worried her, except perhaps that she had a great respect for Mr. Henderson, and she liked to think there was genuine harmony among the staff at the Centre.

But she was just a little puzzled about Iris. How had she managed to break through his reserve? Perhaps now he would loosen up a little in other ways.

But there was no sign of his doing so in the Theatre the next day, and Netta found she was becoming more and more interested in him, more and more concerned for him. He seemed, somehow, outside of things, and she wanted to draw him in.

And so, out of the best of all motives, she began to smile at him more readily, to make efforts at conversation and, in general, to make him feel less isolated. She was convinced that he *was* feeling isolated.

There was to be a dance at the hospital in a few days' time. Towards the end of treatment for extensive burns with which Jerry was assisting Roger, and Hugh giving the anaesthetic, Jerry began discussing the coming event.

"I only hope this new band they're getting is a bit better than the last."

"Couldn't be worse, at any rate," Hugh agreed. "You couldn't hear yourself speak, even at the bottom end of the Rec."

"You're going to get off, are you, Netta?" asked Jerry.

She nodded. "Staff Nurse Kelly doesn't dance, so she's not interested in going. The night nurse doesn't dance, either. But in any case nobody gets there until about nine, so after-duty hours is all right. An evening off isn't really necessary."

"No, but don't you girls take about three hours to dress and make up your faces?" joked Jerry.

"Who on earth told you that tale?" she retorted.

She noticed that Roger Henderson hadn't said a word. Taking her courage in both hands, as it were, she said:

"Are you going to the dance, Mr. Henderson?"

Both Hugh and Jerry glanced swiftly from her to Roger, then waited for his reply.

There was a full minute's silence, then Roger said mildly: "I might, Sister. I might."

Hugh eyed him, his eyes over his theatre mask keen and direct.

"Well, that'll shake the foundations, I'm sure," he murmured, lowering his eyes to his patient.

Jerry merely shrugged his lean shoulders and said nothing.

But Hugh said to her afterwards: "You do stick your neck out, don't you?"

She gave him a puzzled look. "I don't know what you mean, Hugh."

"Well, I ask you! You try to be nice and friendly, ask him if he's coming to the dance, and all you get is: "I might, Sister, I might." What kind of an answer is that?"

"I don't see anything wrong with it," Netta answered doggedly.

"You don't? Well, I call it downright supercilious and unfriendly. I tell you, Netta, you're just wasting your time trying to be nice to him."

"I don't agree," she said firmly. "It's never a waste of time being nice to people."

Hugh said he just didn't like to see someone like Netta snubbed and hurt, but as she didn't feel either, she dismissed his advice, though she appreciated his motive for giving it. Why shouldn't she have asked Mr. Henderson if he were going to the dance? It was the first of the season. Nobody even knew whether he was interested in dancing. Unless perhaps Iris Leighton did. But nobody had been able to draw Iris out regarding the surgeon at all, oddly enough.

"I'd have thought she'd be only too ready to crow about her "conquest", said Elva. "But she hasn't said a word. I wonder why?"

"There might be nothing in it, and she doesn't want to crow too soon," Netta suggested. "Whether he comes to the dance or not, we shall just have to wait and see."

But the time crept to ten-thirty on the night, and there was no sign either of Iris or Roger Henderson. Netta didn't know why she should feel so disappointed, but she was. She danced mostly with Jerry, as usual, and occasionally with Hugh.

"I wonder if there's anything on in theatre," she said to Jerry as they danced.

"It would be almost surprising if there wasn't," he said, giving her a puzzled look. "But what brought that up?"

"Oh, I just wondered."

"Ah! I know," Jerry said suddenly. "You're wondering if the great man himself is coming to the dance, aren't you?"

"Well, I——" She affected a casual shrug. "I just wondered, you know, if he would. Iris Leighton isn't here, either."

"Dear, dear," mocked Jerry. "I wonder where they are and what they're up to?"

Netta felt her cheeks grow warm. "All right, Jerry Somers, there's no need to be so funny," she said, laughing a little shamefacedly.

But the next minute Jerry let out a soft whistle. "Talk of the devil, here they come, both of them. And oh, boy, look at Iris! Dressed to kill."

Netta looked. Iris was wearing the most beautiful cocktail dress. The very latest in design and material, it was a breathtaking combination of simplicity and sophistication.

"That must have knocked her back a packet," murmured Jerry. "Not to mention the hair-do."

Iris was tall with a slender figure, and her hair was a rich black which shone with health and vitality. She stood just inside the doorway with Roger and looked nonchalantly around the room, a faint smile on her lips.

"She looks like the cat that's been at the cream," said Jerry.

With a feeling she couldn't put a name to, Netta's glance went to Roger, looking the very personification of the smart man about town in his dinner jacket. Standing together, there was no doubt about it, they looked a very distinguished pair, Iris and he.

"They look as though they've been out to dinner or something," she said, a hint of envy creeping into her voice.

"Yes. You can almost see the pair of them licking their lips," laughed Jerry.

They began to dance then, and there was no doubt about it whatsoever. Roger Henderson danced very well indeed, and he was well matched by Iris. It became evident that he had no intention of having any "duty dances". He danced one number after the other with Iris.

"There you are," Hugh said to Netta as they sat recovering their breath after a quickstep. "I told you, didn't I? He doesn't need either your interest, your sympathy or your friendship."

She watched for a moment as Iris and Roger danced a slow foxtrot with elegance and expertise.

"Yes, Hugh, you told me," she said, with a sigh, and couldn't help adding: "several times."

But towards the end of the evening she happened to be standing alone. Hugh had asked Elva to dance, and Jerry was dancing with someone else, too. All at once Roger Henderson stood before her, a faint smile on his face.

"Would you care to dance, Sister? Or is it Netta on these occasions?"

She doubted whether she managed to hide the surprise she felt.

She gave him her hand. "Netta it is—and I'd love to dance."

It was a waltz. And dancing it with him was like floating on air. For a little while Netta just gave herself up to the sheer enjoyment of it. Jerry was rather an indifferent dancer, Hugh was inclined to hold his partner too closely. But dancing with Roger Henderson was a perfect dream. She wanted it never to end.

"Are you enjoying the dance?" he asked, however, during the first encore.

She blinked and smiled up at him, then said, with sudden impishness:

"To tell you the truth, I thought you were never going to ask me."

It was only when she saw his raised eyebrows that she realized what she had said. He had meant was she enjoying the evening, of course, not this particular dance. In any case, she had not even been aware of wanting him to ask her to dance.

He gave a slow smile. "Well, well! I wish I'd known. But every time I saw you, you were already dancing."

She became aware of his hand, much bigger than her own, and cool and strong, as it enveloped hers, and his arm half around her waist. So she was wasting her time, was she? He was one of the most attractive men she had met in a long time. Was it possible he had been at the hospital for over six months? A thrill of excitement bubbled up inside her and gave a sparkle to her eyes and her smile.

"I was only joking, of course. But I'm glad you did ask me to dance before the evening was over. You dance so beautifully."

There was slight amusement in his smile as he looked down at her.

"You pay the most delightful compliments. Now I know why you're so popular."

"Oh but really, Mr.—er, Mr.——"

"Roger's the name under these circumstances, don't you think?"

She could have laughed out loud. As it was, the demon which seemed to be inside her tonight caused her to give a slight giggle.

"Do you know, Mr. Henderson—sir—I've always wanted to call you Roger."

She was flirting with him outrageously, she knew it. Or at least, she felt sure he would think so. Then, as though responding to her mood, he said the most surprising thing.

"You know, you're asking for trouble. You're simply asking to be taken out of here to some dark corner and kissed until you struggle for breath."

She gulped. "The very suggestion makes me breathless!"

The lights were lowered for the waltz, as often happened. Suddenly Netta found herself being propelled out of the door of the recreation room into the corridor outside. Another door led outside the building altogether.

"Where are we going?" she queried, half laughing, feeling a little uneasy.

"For a little walk."

It was almost pitch dark. She stumbled, and he put his arm about her to steady her. There was something unreal about what was happening. She couldn't believe that this was the same person who had been so withdrawn, so aloof, and so much on his dignity in the Theatre. This slipping out of the ballroom on occasions like these was more the kind of thing the student nurses and medical students might do, and often did.

"Well now, let's see, shall we?" she heard him murmur.

The next moment he had caught her in his arms and his lips were on hers, in a kiss Netta would remember all her life. It was tender and at the same time possessive, gentle, and yet demanding and a little cruel.

Never before had Netta been kissed like this. And everything within her responded to him, responded joyously and with rapturous abandon.

When at last he let her go, she was breathless indeed. And she was head-over-heels in love with him.

## CHAPTER THREE

HOW long she stood there after Roger Henderson had left her, Netta did not know. It might have been half a lifetime, it might have been only a few minutes. Neither time nor anything else mattered. She wanted to laugh and to cry. *Or, Roger, Roger, I love you*, her heart chanted. That he had disappeared, that he had left her standing there was of no consequence whatever to her at this moment. She was lost in the wonder of revelation. She was in love. Gloriously, marvelously in love.

The door of the building opened suddenly and discharged two laughing couples. It slammed shut after them, rousing Netta from her rosy, trance-like state. She went back inside and drifted into the ballroom again, her eyes searching, in a vague sort of way, for Roger.

But it was Jerry who loomed up in front of her. "Where on earth have you been?"

She looked at him half-stupidly. "Oh, just outside for some air."

Jerry frowned at her. "Hugh said you went with Henderson. Are you all right?"

She laughed. "Of course I'm all right. Actually, Roger came in again. Is he here?"

Her gaze wandered around the room again. What happened to him? Why did he sort of run away?

Jerry eyed her expressively. "So it's Roger, is it? Since when?"

Her gave swivelled back to him. "I don't know what you mean. It's his name, isn't it? I can't keep on calling him *Mr.* Henderson—and I don't like just surnames."

She must keep what she had discovered to herself. No one must know about this wonderful thing which lay quivering in the warmth of her heart. She must guard it, cherish it.

The band was playing a quickstep. Jerry caught her up and led her on to the dance floor.

"Does he know you call him Roger?" he asked sceptically.

She stared at him blankly for a second. "Eh?" Then she remembered. "He asked me to, as a matter of fact. When we were dancing. And he called me Netta."

"Really? And is this the beginning of a beautiful friendship?"

She eyed him a little incredulously, then began to laugh, the joy inside her bubbling to the surface.

"Heavens, Jerry, don't be daft!"

In comparison to what she felt, the words "beautiful friendship" were absurd. But her answer appeared to satisfy Jerry. He swung her round as if he had just been given some good news, and for the rest of the evening, took possession of her. From time to time Netta searched the dancers for sight of Roger, but he appeared to have vanished completely. There was no sign, either, of Iris, and Netta experienced her first tiny stab of pain. But her joy in the discovery of her love swamped that feeling for the time being like a tidal wave, leaving her exhilarated beyond measure.

She was completely unaware of the effect she was having on Jerry until he walked with her to where her car was parked, then stood for a moment to say goodnight.

She had her back to the car door, and he imprisoned her there, looking into her face.

"Darling, you look positively brilliant," he said in a soft voice. "What's got into you?"

She smiled. "Nothing. At least, nothing in particular."

What else could she say? She couldn't possibly tell him. She didn't want to tell him. She didn't want to tell anybody.

Jerry bent his head and kissed her on the lips. "What about that show we promised ourselves? Your next day off? We'll make a special "do" of it, shall we?"

"Yes, all right, Jerry. Day after tomorrow or next week—Friday. Take your choice."

"I'll take both," he said promptly. "And you'd better watch out. I'm likely to devour you—in one swallow."

She laughed, her happiness finding expression. "Silly! Better let me go now, Jerry. Elva and Hugh are bearing down on us."

"Damn Elva and Hugh," he murmured, his lips finding hers again.

Netta remained passive for a brief while, then the memory of Roger and the way he had kissed her came back with renewed intensity. She stirred.

"Jerry—please——"

He put his head back and looked at her. "What's the matter?"

"Nothing. I—just want to get home now, that's all."

He put his hands in his pockets and shrugged his thin shoulders, but she could see he was hurt.

Impulsively, she put out her hand and grasped his arm.

"I'm sorry, Jerry. I—feel tired all at once, that's all. See you day after tomorrow, eh? I'll wait until you call for me."

He nodded and his grin appeared again. "Yeah, O.K., beautiful."

He really was awfully sweet, Netta thought to herself as she unlocked the car door and slipped into the driving seat, then released the lock of the passenger side. It was time he got himself a real girl-friend. One he could really love, who could love him.

"Well, well, so you found her, did you?" came Hugh's voice. He pressed his face to the side window, and she wound it down. "What happened, Netta? Did he get fresh?"

"I don't know what you're talking about."

"You don't? That's a laugh!"

"Stow it, Hugh," said Jerry. "It's no business of yours what Netta does." He pushed his way to the window. "Goodnight, sweetheart. Mind how you go."

Elva got in beside her and Netta drove off. "Enjoy it, Elva?" she asked.

"Not bad. It had its moments." Netta didn't ask her what she meant, and Elva went on: "I noticed Iris and Mr. Henderson didn't stay very long."

"No?" Netta steered carefully round the corner on to the main road. "He's an absolutely wonderful dancer."

Elva said she had noticed that, too. "Took you out for some air, did he?" she added.

"That's right."

"I'm surprised at you, Netta."

"Surprised? Why are you?"

"Well—it didn't seem fair to Jerry."

Netta laughed shortly. "Oh, really, Elva! Jerry and I are only friends. We're not engaged or anything. You don't need me to remind you of that, surely?"

Elva didn't speak for a moment, then she said quietly: "You know, Netta, I think it's high time you came down out of the clouds."

"What on earth do you mean?"

Elva gave a little exasperated sigh. "Can't you see the man's in love with you?"

"Oh, nonsense, Elva. You don't know Jerry as I do. He's fond of me, as I am of him, but he's not in love with me. If he had been, he would have told me. One thing Jerry isn't—and that's shy."

Elva made no reply, and Netta, still nurturing thoughts of Roger, lapsed into her own rosy silence.

When Netta entered Theatre the next morning an operation was already in progress. Her eyes went immediately to the tall figure of Roger at the operating table, and from him to the intravenous stand and the blood transfusion which was being given. The emergency was a serious one, by the look of things. She instructed the day nurses to relieve the night staff, with the exception of the instrument nurse, then went to Sister Jones's desk situated in the centre of the unit, just behind the X-ray department.

"What's in Theatre, Sister?" Netta asked her.

Sister Jones pushed the patient's notes towards her. "There you are, Sister. Read it for yourself. Boy of fourteen, admitted as emergency appendix, but obviously there's something else. Enjoy the dance last night?"

"Yes thanks. And you?"

Sister Jones answered absently, and Netta's attention was already given to the notes on the patient who was on the operating table.

"Thank you, Sister," she murmured, and made her way back to the theatre.

She put on a mask and gown and went into the theatre and stood beside the dirty side of the table. It was the rule that instrument nurses never changed over in the middle of an operation, but in this instance she thought help might be needed. For a minute or two Netta watched in silence. Jerry was assisting, Bob Griffiths giving the anaesthetic, and all were concentrating on what they were doing. The muscle layers and peritoneum had been divided and the opening of the peritoneal cavity reached. Then suddenly there was an exclamation from Jerry.

"Lord above! Look at that."

Swiftly, he reached for swabs and the night staff nurse put more in his reach. Blood-stained fluid was in the cavity in abundance. Anticipating that Roger might want to aspirate, Netta sent one of the student nurses to the preparation room for a syringe and herself replenished the saline in each of the bowls in turn.

When the nurse returned with the syringe, Roger said, without looking up:

"Thank you, Sister."

She had not known that he was aware of her presence. Jerry, it seemed, hadn't been until Roger spoke. Then he glanced up swiftly.

"Ah, good morning, Sister dear. And how are you this fine morning?"

She didn't answer. None would be expected, and she was concentrating on the next stage of the operation. Jerry's remark meant little. It certainly did not mean that he wasn't paying sufficient attention to his job. Jerry was one of those surgeons who could chatter away with ease, and at the same time have his mind fully on what he was doing, no matter how intricate or important.

But Roger said with quiet authority: "Could you cut out the chatter, if you don't mind, Somers?"

46

"Oh, sure, sure," Jerry said equably.

Knowing how easily Jerry could cover up his real feelings, at times, however, she thought it probable that he might be just a little resentful of Roger's remark. She glanced at Roger swiftly, but his gaze was riveted to the site of the operation. He was not in the best of moods this morning, she reflected. Then she turned her attention determinedly to where his own was directed. The previous evening and what had happened both inside and outside the recreation room threatened to intrude into her thoughts more than they should.

The remaining fluid in the peritoneal cavity having been aspirated, the reasons for the boy's pain and collapse became startlingly apparent.

"I'm afraid there's only one thing for it," murmured Roger. "Resection of the small intestine. You agree, Somers?"

Jerry considered for a moment, then he nodded. "Only thing you can do. After all, with somewhere around twenty feet of it the poor blighter won't miss an odd foot or so."

"Precisely," Roger said drily.

Netta couldn't help contrasting the two men— Roger, the proverbial 'man of few worls'; Jerry, the talker. Roger, the enigma; Jerry, the uncomplicated. It seemed incredible that last night—— Again, she checked her wayward thoughts.

"Unusual case this," Jerry went on, unable to keep silent for long, in spite of his chief's previous irritability. "Would you say the condition is congenital?"

"I should say so, yes."

"Due, maybe to a constriction or even a smaller mesentery. Wouldn't be noticed in the lad's early life, only when his innards began to grow."

"Exactly."

"Hope he makes a good recovery, anyhow."

Netta went out. Jerry was a pet, but if he once decided to start talking about last night——

She worked for a while in the preparation room, making up packs, checking those that were there, and now she could not help her thoughts from straying to Roger. What would he be thinking this morning? What had possessed him to kiss her like that—or even at all? Had it meant anything to him? But of course not. It had been just one of those impulses a man was given to at times. But whether it had meant anything to him or not, nothing could take away her inward glow of happiness. She had felt on top of the world before this. Now she was almost bursting with a kind of joy and excitement. She had never felt like this in her life before, and it was a wonderful, glorious feeling.

She was wondering whether the operation was finished when the night staff nurse came into the room.

"Sister, Mr. Henderson wants to speak to you," she told her.

Netta's heart gave a sudden jerk. "Oh, Oh, very good, Nurse. Now don't you linger. Off you go. You must be worn out."

There was no Theatre Sister's office. Roger was sitting on the anaesthetist stool, but at the sight of Netta he stood up.

"You wanted to speak to me?" she asked a little shyly, but smiling up at him.

"Er—yes, Sister." He folded his arms and eyed her without the merest hint of a smile in return for hers. "I—just wanted to say here and now that I'm—sorry about last night. It's—not the sort of thing I make a habit of doing, and I'd be obliged if you would accept my apology and then forget the whole regrettable incident."

She blinked. "I—I didn't suppose you did make a habit of it, er—Mr. Henderson. But—but there's no need whatever for you to apologize. I mean, I——" she faltered. She had been going to say that she didn't mind in the least, but suddenly realized how that would sound.

"You mean you accept my apology?" he prompted stiffly.

"Why—yes, of course."

He gave her an uncertain, half-incredulous look, then turned and left the theatre. He almost collided with Hugh, who was just coming in. Hugh gave Netta a mocking smile.

"What gives with the Great White Chief? Trying to explain away his behavior—his extraordinary behavior of last night?"

Netta eyed him absently for a moment. Her thoughts and feelings were in a turmoil. She wanted nothing more than to go somewhere private where she could sort them out. But she wouldn't be able to, she knew that. There was the theatre to be cleaned up, there were sounds of activity all around, any second, perhaps, another case would be wheeled in.

"I don't know what you're talking about," she answered Hugh. "Did you want to see me about something? If not——"

"It'll keep," he said easily, still smiling.

Netta moved swiftly about her work, urging on her nurses in the business of clearing up, giving a hand with the cleaning and re-packing of the instruments ready for autoclaving. The warm glow she had had, the delicious thrill of being in love was now like a light flickering on and off uncertainly. She had rather Roger had said nothing. She hadn't expected him to feel the same way that she did, but she had thought, had hoped in a vague sort of way that there would be something between them. Some special bond, a hint of—friendship, perhaps. But obviously he deeply regretted whatever impulse had prompted him to——

The entrance of Sister Jones put her thoughts to flight. "Multiple injuries, Sister. Another boy, I'm afraid. Knocked down by a bus on his way to school."

"Right, Sister."

Netta gave instructions with regard to the operation packs which would be needed and delegated other tasks to the various nurses, then began to scrub up to act as instrument nurse herself. She never ceased to be amazed at the speed with which the theatre was prepared for each operation in the new Centre. In the old theatre, all the sterilizing had been done by boiling, sterile cloths had to be laid out on all the instrument and suture trolleys separately. Now, this was all streamlined. A 'dirty-nurse' simply untied the outer wrapping of the packs and held them out to the instrument nurse, her hands underneath and the outer wrapping hanging down all round. The instrument nurse picked up the inner, sterile pack and laid this, cover and instruments together on her trolleys. Needles and sutures were ready threaded in transparent polythene packets.

She was pulling on her gloves when Jerry came in already wearing his theatre cap and mask.

"Everything under control, Netta?"

"I think so. Are you doing it?"

He nodded and began to scrub. "This looks like being one of those days. A man has just been brought in who's fallen from a height of around sixty feet or more. It's a wonder he's still living. Be a job for the E.N.T., Orthopaedics *and* Ophthalmologist, most likely. The man's a horrible sight. But for the knowledge of what *can* be done—— Well, I'd just want to chuck up the job."

Netta knew exactly how he felt. Every now and then one became sickened by the sight of so much suffering, so many mangled bodies. But not often, anl not for long. Nurses and doctors looked continually to the future. Their concern was with healing, what *could* be done, what the patient was going to be like tomorrow, next week, a picture of the man or woman walking out of the gates cured, of a child running and shouting. Their working day was too full to allow personal reactions to linger.

"When do you surgeons eat?" she asked. "Did you have any breakfast?"

"Cup of coffee, that's all. This won't take long, then I shall get away to eat."

"And what about—Mr. Henderson?"

He turned and grinned at her. "Roger, you mean? I imagine he'll hand over to Steve. It's his case. But of course he'll want to be in on it to some extent. You look like having a theatre full."

Jerry was right. Three consultants were called in to the next operation. The patient had fallen from the scaffolding surrounding a block of flats which was being built, and had sustained severe head and other injuries.

"Well, there don't appear to be any chest or abdominal injuries, thank heaven," said the orthopaedic consultant, as he and the other consultants and Steve Munro grouped around the view boxes examining the X-ray plates.

"First thing to do is attend to that frontal region, I imagine, don't you, gentlemen?"

The other two agreed with the E.N.T. specialist, and after some further consultation the programme was decided upon.

The orthopaedic consultant turned to Netta, who had been standing a little distance away.

"Is that all right with you, Sister? In about a quarter of an hour or so?"

"Yes, sir. Certainly."

The treatment this patient would receive in theatre this morning would be only the beginning, of course. He would remain dangerously ill for

51

weeks or months. Much would depend on the extent of the brain damage.

As Jerry had said, it was one of those days. Just as an operation had been in progress when Netta had come on duty, Roger was operating again when the night nurse came on. Netta had been off duty for a short period during the afternoon. Whether or not Roger had had any off duty she did not know. If he had, it could only have been a very short period.

It had been an odd day for Netta. Since Roger had made his apology she had not been quite sure how she had felt. She knew only that each time Roger entered the theatre her world became a special place. She loved him. She would always love him. Her bubbly feeling might have gone, she might be feeling a little bruised, a part of her might be in a peculiar kind of pain because he did not love her, but that precious thing still lay secreted in her heart.

At nine o'clock he pulled off his mask and gloves at the end of a two-hour operation and sighed. Then her heart leapt as he said to her in a quiet, gentle voice:

"It seems quite a long time since this morning, Sister, doesn't it?"

"Yes, sir. Yes, Mr. Henderson, it does," she answered breathlessly. Then: "You've been on longer than any of us. Can I make you some coffee?"

A nurse came forward to untie the tapes of his gown. He thanked her and discarded it into her hands. He looked at Netta and was about to say something, but Jerry, who had been helping to lift the patient back on to the stretcher-trolley, now came towards them.

"Netta, my girl, it's time you went home. You've had one hell of a day. We all have. I'm going to drive you straight home."

Almost before Jerry had finished speaking Roger had gone. Netta pulled off her own regalia wearily.

"Jerry, there's no point in you driving me home when I've got my own car outside."

"I'm driving you home in *your* car," he insisted. "Then I shall walk back." He grinned. "The exercise will do me good, seeing that I haven't had enough all day."

She made no further protest. He was being particularly kind and thoughtful, and she appreciated it, but she did so want to be alone. This afternoon in her short off-duty period Mrs. Morney had come up to the flat to ask her advice about a pain in her back. As Netta had just made a pot of tea, there was nothing she could do but ask her landlady to share a cup with her. But Mrs. Morney had been in an unusually talkative mood, and by the time she had gone it was time for Netta to get ready to go back on duty.

She sat back in silence while Jerry drove her the short journey to the flat. She wanted nothing more than to creep into bed and her own little private world in which there was just Roger, the way he looked, the way he spoke. Just he and she in the cosy world of her thoughts.

Jerry brought the car to a stop with a sudden application of the brake, jerking her upright.

"Sorry," he grinned. "I'm not used to your car yet. Poor you, I believe you were almost asleep."

She reached out for the door. "Thanks a lot, Jerry. If you could do one thing more for me—drive it into the garage——"

"Yes, sure."

She halted. "Are you—coming up, Jerry?"

He pursed his lips for a moment. "I might—just for a minute. But I won't stay long. You go on up. I'll follow. It—er—is all right with your Mrs. Thingummy, is it?"

53

Netta assured him it was, then mounted the stairs. Elva was in, sitting beside the window with a book. She put it down and gave a long yawn as Netta entered.

"Hello. Honestly, the most dreary programmes these days on television. Was that Jerry I saw in the car?"

"Yes. He's coming up."

"But how ridiculous. I mean—is he walking back?"

"It isn't really far."

"No, but——" She broke off as Jerry came in.

Netta sat down on her own divan. Jerry looked at her. "Netta's had one hell of day," he said to Elva. "What about strolling back with me to pick my car up, Elva? Then we could pop into the Cheshire Cheese. I've a feeling Netta just wants to crawl into bed."

Elva looked from one to the other, then with a slight shrug, jumped up.

"Suits me, Jerry. Just give me one minute to powder my hair and comb my nose, if you know what I mean, and I'll be right with you."

Netta breathed a long, slow, inward sigh of relief. At last she was going to be left alone with her thoughts, in that blessed place where Roger was waiting and where her love could be taken out and contemplated in an eternity of leisure and peace. She scarcely heard them say goodnight. When they had gone she took off her shoes and stretched out on her bed for a while. Then presently she had a bath and slipped between the sheets, her mind reaching out for sleep.

But this rosy first phase of love could not possibly last for long, and the next two days were painful ones indeed. Roger's name was being linked with that of Iris Leighton. Netta had been so much in the clouds she had all but forgotten their appearance together at the dance.

"One swallow doesn't make a summer, anyway," she said to Elva, unwilling to believe that there was anything of a lasting nature between them.

"You forget he was waiting for her that night in the Cheshire Cheese," Elva told her. "And from all accounts they were out together last night, too. But why not? It only goes to show that he's human, after all."

Netta looked down into her cup. "Yes, but why Iris? You said yourself how ruthless she can be. In fact, you were feeling sorry for him—in advance—not so long ago."

"And you, if I remember rightly, stated that our senior surgical officer was well able to take care of himself," Elva retorted. Then she laughed. "Are you disappointed that he's not quite the shy, lonely figure you suddenly decided he was that evening in the Cheshire Cheese? You know, I do believe——"

But Elva had suddenly become serious. She broke off and rose abruptly to her feet and went out of the room. Netta was not sorry. She did not want to go on talking about Roger and Iris. And now, instead of wanting to be alone to allow her thoughts to dwell upon him, she wanted to be alone to weep. What was she going to do? How was she going to go on working alongside him day after day feeling like this about him? She couldn't go on hiding her feelings for ever. Sooner or later she would give herself away. That very afternoon Hugh asked her what was the matter.

He strolled into the theatre as she was scrubbing up for the treatment of burns, one of those occasions when it was impossible for her to walk away from a conversation. He bent his head and peered into her face as she scrubbed her hands and arms.

"Hello, hello, where have all those stars gone from your eyes? Jerry not proposed yet—or have you got someone else lined up who's equally backward?"

She felt her color rise. "Oh, for goodness' sake, Hugh! Is that all you can think about?"

He shrugged. "No, not quite. I'm just waiting for my chance to nip in, as it were."

"Oh, really, Hugh, I'm not in the mood for——"

She glanced up at the clock. There were times when this five minutes scrubbing time was more like five hours. How she wished he would go away. But he leaned against the next basin, his arms folded as though he intended remaining there for ever.

"As a matter of fact, you promised me a date some time."

She breathed heavily. "Hugh, do you mind?" she muttered, giving him an angry look. "I don't like this kind of conversation in front of my nurses."

His eyes opened wide and looked swiftly around. "Darling, there isn't a soul in sight."

She glanced up at the clock again, and the second hand gave a jump forward to the half-hour. With relief she rinsed the soap from her hands and arms and turned off the taps with her elbow. This done she could move away from him.

But how much longer would it be before other people, too, noticed that she was not quite so happy as she used to be? How on top of the world she had been a few short weeks ago! Maybe she had been too happy. She had heard it said that life could be like that.

She was glad to get off duty, yet when she did she found time dragging heavily on her hands. It was no longer a pleasure to let herself indulge in thoughts of Roger. The longing to be loved by him was already becoming intense. She could not bear to be in the flat alone, so when she had changed and had some tea she got into her car again and went for a drive. Whether Hugh was off duty, she did not know, but she almost wished she were seeing him. Hugh could be aggravating at times, but anything would be preferable to being alone.

It was her day off the following day, the day Jerry had planned to take her to a show and a meal afterwards. He called early and they had tea together first. She had put on a dress that she knew he liked, a frilly, feminine one, and she couldn't help wondering, foolishly, how Roger's taste went in the way of women's fashion. But she tried to put Roger out of her mind. Jerry was the person who mattered tonight. He was in particularly good form and was grateful for that, grateful, too, for his friendship.

He was also particularly affectionate this evening, showing this in a dozen different ways. The way he helped her in and out of the car, guided her up the steps of the theatre, linked her arm and grasped her hand during the performance, and in the marked attention he paid her. But he kept up such a flow of conversation that it was not until they were driving home after the meal that she remembered Elva's words the evening of the dance.

Netta frowned to herself. Was it true? Was Jerry really in love with her? She closed her eyes in a moment of despair. Oh, no. Please God, let it not be so. Why was life so difficult all at once?

Jerry pulled the car into the lay-by as he often did, but this time Netta wished he hadn't. Should she ask him to drive her straight to the flat? But he made no attempt to put his arm around her even and so she relaxed and waited for him to pull out his cigarette case.

But instead, she felt his hand reach out for hers.

He found it and held it for a moment, then began, in a quiet voice:

"There's something I've been meaning to tell you, Netta. And this is as good a time and place as any."

She turned her head and looked at him. This didn't sound like the prelude to a declaration of love. Perhaps Elva had been mistaken. In fact—the thought suddenly occurred to her—perhaps he wanted to end their friendship. Perhaps he was beginning to prefer Elva's company and tonight was something in the nature of a farewell.

"What is it, Jerry? Something important?"

"Yeah. It's this, Netta. I want to get married. That's the plain truth. And I—well, I want to marry you."

## CHAPTER FOUR

HER startled gaze met his. Then a smile curved his lips and his eyebrows shot up a little comically. She relaxed.

"Oh, Jerry, you're joking! For a minute, I thought you were serious."

His eyebrows came back to normal. "But sweetheart, I *am* serious. I tried to lead up to it a week or so ago, but——"

She averted her head. "Jerry, I—don't know what to say. I had no idea you felt like this. I mean—we've known each other for such a long time now, and——"

"Exactly. And although we've had arguments we've never once seriously quarrelled. I think we'd make a go of it. I'm—not much of a one for making pretty speeches, as you know, Netta, but there's one thing I haven't mentioned yet. I—guess I'm in love with you——"

Netta slumped in her seat. The irony of life! That after all this time Jerry should be in love with her without her having even an inkling. She simply did not know what to say to him. He reached for her other hand and held both in his.

"Well, what do you think, Netta?" he asked, with a brightness which did not sound quite natural.

"I—I don't know, Jerry," she said, distressed.

He laughed briefly. "Don't say—this is so sudden."

"Well, it is rather. As you say, we've been friends for such a long time, and we've never been what you might call romantic about each other, have we?"

"I suppose not, but—well, I thought——" He broke off and gave an enormous sigh. "But what's the good of talking? It's obvious you don't feel the same way as I do, otherwise we shouldn't *be* talking."

"Jerry, I'm sorry——"

"Oh, don't apologize," he said with exaggerated casualness. "If it's no use, it's no use, and that's all there is to it."

Netta felt utterly miserable. She couldn't say she loved him if she didn't, but she didn't want to hurt him, neither did she want to lose his friendship.

"But we can still be friends, Jerry, can't we?"

He leaned his arms on the steering wheel and shook his head slowly.

"No. Not in the same way. I simply couldn't. You know, we couldn't have gone on like this indefinitely, surely you can see that, Netta? Platonic friendship can last only for so long—until one of the party falls in love. Something was bound to happen. One or the other of us would have either fallen in love with somebody else or—well, what *has* happened."

He turned and looked at her and saw the anxious expression on her face.

His grin appeared briefly. "Don't look so worried. It's true I'm in love with you, but I shan't go into a decline or commit hari-kari or anything like that. I'll survive—I expect—but only if I don't see you outside hospital. Sorry, Netta, but—well, I'm sure you'll understand."

"Yes, of course," she said bleakly.

There was a heavy silence for a minute or two, then Jerry switched on the engine and started up the car. He dropped her off outside the flat.

"No use my asking you to come up, I suppose?" she asked.

He shook his head, then eyed her, his expression tender, and a twisted smile which wrenched at her heart.

"You're sure it's no use, Netta? You don't see yourself as Mrs. Jerry Somers?"

"Oh, Jerry, I wish——"

But he held up his hand. "Don't get upset again. I only wanted to make sure. 'Night then, beautiful —and the best of luck always."

He grasped her hard by the shoulders and brought his lips down on hers fiercely for a moment, then let her go.

"All right, my dear, off you go."

She gave a quivering high and, with a heavy heart, opened the car door and went into the house. Before she had closed the front door behind her, his car roared up the street to fade into nothingness, leaving her sad and depressed beyond measure.

Elva was in. Netta reflected how much her life had changed since Elva had moved in with her. It had seemed so normal, so acceptable at the time, because life had been so uncomplicated. Now she just wanted to be alone. She was too unhappy for bright, ordinary chatter.

"Hello," Elva greeted her. "Jerry not coming up tonight, then?"

"No, not tonight."

Netta took off her coat and hung it in the large cupboard which served as a wardrobe, and hoped Elva would sense that she didn't want to talk. But her hopes were in vain.

"Something wrong?" came the question.

Netta sighed. She supposed she might as well tell Elva. She would have to know some time.

"Nothing's wrong in particular—except that Jerry and I have reached a sort of crisis."

Elva stared at her. "A crisis!"

Netta sank on to her divan. "You can get ready to say "I told you so", Elva. Jerry, as you said, is in love with me and wants to marry me."

"And you've turned him down," came the swift, half query, half statement.

Netta rose again and began to undress. "If you must put it so crudely—yes."

"You're crazy!"

Netta's eyes filled with tears. Her sense of loss was acute. And loving Roger, who outside the theatre scarcely knew of her existence, was pain enough itself. She tightened her lips, and with her back to Elva, peeled off her stockings then hung up her dress and put on her dressing gown without speaking.

She could feel Elva's eyes following her as she went to the door.

"You going to have a bath?" Elva asked quietly.

"Yes."

And in the sanctity of hot water and steam Netta faced squarely, and accepted, though not without sadness, this inevitable change which had so suddenly come about in her relationship with

Jerry. It had to come, and now that it had, she must accept it.

Her desire to weep had been largely self-pity. But though she emerged from the bathroom dry-eyed and more in control of her emotions the sadness on Jerry's account and on Roger's, mingled to form one tremendous ache in her heart.

When she went back into the flat Elva, too, was in her dressing gown. There was a heavy silence for a minute, then Elva said:

"Netta, I'm sorry if I was tactless just now. You didn't know how Jerry felt, I realize that. All the same, you were fond of him, and it can't have been easy for you to—have to tell him——"

"No, it wasn't."

"Are you—going to go on seeing each other?"

Netta shook her head. "Jerry doesn't want to, and under the circumstances it's best. I shall miss him, of course, but there you are, these things happen."

"Was Jerry very cut up?"

Netta gave a slight smile. "Hard to tell. You know Jerry. Takes everything with a grin."

"That doesn't mean he can't be hurt," Elva said rather sharply.

Netta looked at her. "I know," she said quietly.

After this they lapsed into silence. Netta had the feeling that Elva's sympathies were heavily weighed in Jerry's favor, as if she, Netta, was to blame for what had happened. Netta frowned suddenly. Was she to blame? Had she been blind, led Jerry on to fall in love with her? Without realizing it, of course. Perhaps she should have been more sensitive, perhaps she had been too wrapped up in her own froth of happiness and success, career-wise. It was odd. If she had thought of their break-up one day, at all, she had somehow visualized them both falling in love with someone else. But life, it seemed, was not quite as simple as that.

The days fused on with another in a haze of preparing theatre, clearing up theatre, autoclaving and checking. Jerry became elusive, little more than a white-clad figure who came and went, who stood gowned and masked at the operating table, sometimes operating, sometimes assisting. He did not visit the flat, but once or twice she caught a glimpse of him in the plaster room chatting with Elva. She tried, in vain, to forget that she was in love with Roger, and of course, sooner or later it gradually became known that Jerry and she were no longer the bosom companions they had formerly been.

"What's gone wrong with you and Jerry, then?" came from Hugh. "Has he popped the question at last and you've turned him down?"

"No, it was the other way round," she told him tartly.

He laughed. "Ask a silly question and you get a silly answer, eh?"

"That's right."

"Ah well, it was bound to come. You can have a platonic friendship *as well as* the other kind, but not instead of, in my opinion."

"Very sound philosophy, Hugh."

He eyed her shrewdly. "I must say you're not your usual sparkling self these days, though. What about coming to the Cheshire Cheese tonight? I could do with a bit of a lift myself."

"If I'm not very sparkling, I shouldn't have thought you'd get much of a lift in my company."

He smiled. "Then you'd be wrong. Being in your company would give any man a lift—and me, in particular."

She gave him an amused glance. "Really, Hugh, such flattery!" Compliments came oddly from him, somehow, she was not sure why.

He raised one eyebrow. "See? It's done you good already. Now what about tonight? You're off at five, aren't you?"

After a momentary hesitation Netta agreed to his suggestion. It did no good to brood, which she was inclined to do when she stayed in the flat for an evening.

"Thanks, Hugh. I'll see you there, then. Around seven?"

Elva was off duty, too. "Going somewhere special?" Netta asked casually, as Elva, looking particularly smart, stood at the window of the flat, pulling on her gloves.

Elva nodded. "As a matter of fact I'm seeing Jerry. I—hope you don't mind."

"Mind? Heavens, no. Why should I? Is he calling for you?"

"No, I asked him not to. I wasn't sure how you'd feel about it."

Netta fought down a rather empty feeling in the pit of her stomach.

"Look, Elva, if you want to ask Jerry up here, go ahead. Don't mind me. As for your going out together—well, that's fine. It has nothing to do with me, so don't have me on your conscience. Jerry as good as told me that he wouldn't sit around moping. I'm seeing Hugh, anyway, so——"

"Oh, really? Oh, Netta, I'm so glad!"

The relief on Elva's face was unmistakable. Netta couldn't help laughing.

"Look, I'm only meeting him in the Cheshire Cheese. I mean there's nothing in it. Don't go thinking up a romance. It isn't even a question of 'off with the old love, on with the new'—or anything like that."

Netta was at the Cheshire Cheese early. She ordered a glass of sherry and sat down at a small table to wait. She hadn't been here since the evening when Roger had sat waiting for Iris

Leighton. Thinking of that evening Netta hoped, suddenly, that the same thing wouldn't happen tonight. But the thought had no sooner crossed her mind than her heart gave a great leap as he appeared in the doorway.

He looked round the room, then hesitated as he saw Netta. She smiled briefly and he walked towards her.

"Good evening, Netta," he said gravely.

Her lips seemed glued together for one awful moment. "I—good evening. Won't you—sit down?"

"Thank you. You're waiting for someone?"

She nodded. "And you?"

"As a matter of fact, no. But as soon as your—whoever you're waiting for turns up, I'll make myself scarce, of course."

She wanted to protest, to beg him to stay. It seemed incredible that here she was, making such polite, meaningless conversation with Roger of all people. Roger whom she loved so much. They should be talking about things that mattered, getting to know each other, exchanging their views on life and the universe, morality and religion, and a thousand and one other things people did talk about to the person who was going to be closest to them.

She held the stem of her glass tightly and gazed into its golden contents, her lips compressed against the pain in her heart. He didn't love her. To him, she was just someone he knew, someone he had taken outside on some kind of impulse, and kissed her for no other motive.

"You're not looking too happy, Netta." His voice came so gently, she could have wept. "I—understand you and Jerry Somers——"

She could not bear his sympathy, his kindness. "Roger—please, I'd rather not talk about it."

She was sitting facing the door, and to her relief Hugh came in. Roger saw the smile on her face and turned. Then, as soon as it was evident that Hugh was the one she was waiting for, he stood up.

"I'll leave you, then."

Hugh joined her as Roger moved away. He had a peculiar smile on his face, and his glance followed Roger who was making for the door.

"And what did the Big White Chief have to say to you?" he asked.

Netta looked at him with distaste. "Why do you call him that?"

Hugh's brows shot up. "It seems appropriate, that's all."

"I sometimes think you really dislike him—personally, I mean."

Hugh lifted his shoulders in an indifferent shrug. "Oh, I wouldn't say that. But he's so unsociable. He asks to be dubbed. Still, let's talk about something a little more pleasant, shall we?"

She tried to subdue her anger. He wasn't to know she was in love with Roger. And she didn't want him to know, either. She didn't want anyone to know. Hugh began to talk, to tell her about a holiday he had had in Spain. Netta did her best to listen, but she couldn't help thinking of the kindness in Roger's voice as he had asked her about Jerry. How wonderful he would be to the woman he loved. But he had only been handing out ordinary sympathy. He would use that kindly tone to anyone in need of consolation.

"What part of Spain did you go to, then?" Hugh was saying.

She looked at him blankly. "H'm? I'm sorry. I've never been to Spain."

He gave her a half-amused glance. "I asked you just now and you said yes."

"I'm sorry, Hugh," she said again. "I must have said it without thinking."

"You mean you were thinking of something else. Or some*one* else."

"Hugh, I'm——"

He gestured with his hand. "Don't keep apologizing, for goodness' sake, Netta. It's obvious to anyone that you've got something on your mind. Maybe you'd like to talk about it."

She shook her head. "Not really, Hugh. Anyway, why should I unload my troubles on to you? Tell me more about your holiday in Spain. I'd like to go there some time."

By the end of the evening, she was grateful to Hugh. At first she had to force herself to listen to what he was saying, but gradually she became really interested. Though she could now easier forget that she had two arms, two legs and a body than forget Roger for a single instant, at least the pain and the longing she had for him became a little more bearable.

"Thank you so much, Hugh," she said when he saw her to the flat. "It's been a very pleasant evening."

They stood for a moment in the dimly-lit vestibule of the front door of the house. Hugh put one arm about her and lifted up her chin.

"Again soon?"

"If you like."

"Don't sound too enthusiastic, will you?"

"I'm sorry——"

"There you go again!"

"I wonder you want to see me again, Hugh. I haven't been over-bright."

He looked into her face then he bent his head and brought his lips down on hers. She made no protest. She had not the heart, and it was nothing more than a goodnight kiss. But the next moment the memory of Roger's kiss swooped down on her swiftly, and her lips began to tremble. Then Hugh's arms came about her in a stifling embrace and she wanted to sob out loud. But suddenly the door opened and Jerry stood there.

He stopped dead. Hugh released her, and she stood there for a moment, her eyes closed. Nothing seemed to matter any more.

"I beg your pardon, I'm sure," muttered Jerry, and went past them.

Netta heaved a sigh. "I'll say goodnight, Hugh."

He looked at her ruefully. "That's what comes of kissing you on the doorstep!"

She made a movement to pass him. Most of what Hugh said seemed so inconsequential.

He caught at her arm. "What went wrong with you and Jerry? He shuts up like a clam every time I mention the subject."

"In that case, you can hardly expect me to tell you, can you, Hugh? Surely there comes a time in every relationship when you must either go forward or backward, as it were. Nothing stands still."

"Doesn't it? I'm not so sure. You and Jerry certainly stood still for long enough."

She made no reply. That was the way it must have looked to other people, even to herself, but it was obvious to her now that Jerry's feelings had been undergoing a change. She did not want to discuss this with Hugh, however.

She said goodnight to him once more, and again he tried to detain her, to make a definite date with her. But Netta felt she had had enough for one evening.

"Hugh—please! I must go. I'll see you in theatre and we'll fix up something in a day or so."

She pushed open the door Jerry had left unfastened, and made her escape, wanting only to reach the sanctuary of her room. But she had forgotten for the moment that she now shared the flat with Elva. She still hadn't quite got used to going into it and finding someone already there.

She almost flung herself into the room, only to be met with the exclamation:

"Hello, what's the rush? You look as if all the hounds in hell are after you."

Netta recovered herself with an effort and dropped on to her divan. Was she ever to know peace again? Was life ever going to be normal again? She lay on her back, her hands under her head and closed her eyes. *Oh, Roger—Roger—how am I going to live in this vacuum called life unless you love me?*

"Did you see Jerry just now?" intruded Elva's voice.

"Yes, we nearly knocked each other over."

One part of her—she didn't know how—went on making conversation with Elva. The other part reached out, eternally, it seemed, towards Roger. What was he doing at this moment, what was he thinking about, how did he look? Would he ever——

Netta could not quite decide whether she really liked Hugh or not. True, he said derogatory things about Roger from time to time. For that she ought to hate him. All the same, she had reason to be grateful to him during the ensuing weeks.

As if he knew that something was eating the very heart out of her, he asked her out frequently. But for him she might well have spent too many lonely hours in the flat wallowing in misery. Once or twice she was tempted to say no to him so that she could do just that—sit and nurse her wound and think about Roger. But she knew perfectly well that that would have been a sure way to make her life intolerable. She thought of leaving the Centre, getting a Theatre Sister's post in some other town miles away from Witteringham. But at the moment she simply lacked the courage it would take to put him completely out of her life.

Roger's name was now linked firmly with that of Iris. Netta toyed with the idea of trying to get him away from her. After all, until he was married to her, the situation would not be quite hopeless. But she knew she couldn't do a thing like that. It was contrary to her nature, her code of behavior. Besides, if he really loved Iris—— What was the use of a love you had to scheme and cheat to win?

Elva said: "There's no doubt about it. Iris has him fairly hooked," little realizing that she was thrusting a knife into Netta's heart. Then she added: "At the rate you and Hugh are going, it'll be wedding bells for you two before long."

Netta drew in her breath sharply. "Me and Hugh? You must be out of your mind!"

"Why so? I've never seen a man so keen."

"Really, Elva, you're getting too—romantic—for words. Be your age!"

They were watching the dancing at the next social club dance, and Roger was dancing with Iris. Iris herself, at meal times and in the Sisters' sitting room, was continually talking about Roger, and all her off duty, it seemed, was spent in his company. Netta wished with all her heart now that she had not come to the dance. Next time, she told herself, she would offer to relieve the night staff nurse, or even suggest to Hugh that they might go somewhere else. Hugh, at the present moment, had been called to a patient, and Jerry was on duty in Receiving Room at the Centre until eleven o'clock.

But neither Elva nor Netta sat watching the dancing for long. Ben and Joe strolled up to them and asked them to dance. A minute or so later the music changed suddenly to 'Here We Go Round the Mulberry Bush', and with an inward groan, Netta realized it was a Paul Jones, such a feature of these hospital dances. Normally, she liked them, but the thought that she might have to dance with Roger caused her to shrink within herself.

With a grin, Ben released her, and Netta made an attempt to leave the floor and go and sit down. But she was grasped by the hand on either side and pulled willy-nilly into the inner circle of nurses and Sisters. She was praying that when the music stopped Roger woud be at the other side of the room. But he wasn't. He was almost, but not quite, opposite her. Netta side-stepped, her eye on Steve Monro, the orthopaedic surgeon. But Sister Harvey of Recovery, it seemed, had her eye on him, and as if all the Fates intended it, she was face to face with Roger.

Their eyes met for a moment. Then Roger said, in his quiet voice: "Will you dance, Netta?"

Silently, she gave him her hand. It was the sweetest, the most wonderful agony dancing with him again. But she dared not let herself relax and enjoy it too much. After a minute or two she tried to forget that this was Roger whose hand held hers, whose arm was part of the way around her waist. She played a painful game of pretence, and let her gaze flick around the room as if looking for someone.

But this only brought a remark from him she would much rather not have heard.

"Hugh not here tonight? He *is* your latest conquest, I understand," he said lightly.

She couldn't think what to say. For a moment she was silent. He couldn't have said anything to hurt her more. She sought for something to say, even tried to work up an anger against him, but failed.

"What—makes you think I go around making conquests?" she asked. Then she colored as she remembered what had happened at the last hospital dance. Was he judging her by that incident? Did he think she made a habit of allowing her dancing partner to take her outside on the pretext of having some air and then——

He watched the changes of expression on her face. "I don't—think you go around making conquests, I mean. At least, I only meant it as a compliment to you. I know you're not the sort of person to flit lightly from one man to another, but I'm not at all surprised that Hugh stepped in to take Jerry's place."

She stared at him. "But—you don't understand. Nobody does."

Fortunately then, the music changed to the merry-go-round tune again. If it hadn't at that moment Netta feared she would probably have blurted out the whole truth, that she was hopelessly in love with him and would never love anyone else while she lived. She didn't want to dance again. She fought her way through the crowd of dancers ony to run straight into Hugh.

"Hello," he said. "I saw you dancing with Henderson. Has he been saying something to annoy you? You look slightly ruffled."

She took a deep breath. "I sometimes wish I were anywhere but in a hospital community. Everybody thinks they know so much about one's affairs. More than you know yourself."

Hugh smiled. "That's the way it goes. But what did he say?"

"I don't want to talk about it."

"All right. Would you like to dance?"

"Not while it's a Paul Jones."

He laughed and led her to a seat. "I see. You want to avoid undesirable partners. I don't blame you. It's a bit of a hit and miss business at best."

Hugh went on talking, and Netta felt her varying emotions subside a little. But her eyes roved in search of Roger automatically, and when she caught sight of him, he was dancing once more with Iris.

For the rest of the evening Hugh scarcely left her side, but her thoughts continually strayed to

Roger, her eyes seeking him out. When she caught herself at this she told herself to stop behaving like a school girl, but was forced to the conclusion that a woman in love had the same reactions, suffered the same heartache and followed a similar behavior pattern at any age.

Was it the same with men? She doubted it. Jerry had said he was in love with her, but he showed no sign when they met. He went about his work as usual, chatting away during operations in theatre. No outward sign of any inner conflict.

Jerry popped in to the dance as soon as he was free, and during the only time Hugh left the room for a minute he asked Netta to dance.

"Are you sure Elva won't mind?" she asked him.

He gave her a sort of reproving glance. "She's smoking a cigarette, anyway," he said.

Somehow, these days, trivial conversation seemed out of place.

"Are you going to marry Elva?" she asked.

"Jumping the gun rather, aren't you?" he countered. "I could ask you the same about Hugh."

"You could. But you were *wanting* to marry. I wasn't."

He pulled a face. "True. You know, you're a queer girl, Netta."

"Thanks. But why? You've known me long enough to have discovered that before."

He grinned. "How do you know I didn't come to the conclusion ages ago? No, what I mean is: Most women—at least, most women as normal and as good-looking as you—*want* to get married."

"Do they? Maybe you don't know as much about women as you think you do."

"How so?"

"Love means more to most women than merely getting married."

73

"*Some,* but not most," he corrected. "Anyway, it's natural to want both, isn't it? You don't seem to want either."

She didn't reply. Short of giving herself away, there was nothing she could say. Her gaze was directed over Jerry's shoulder, and she suddenly realized she was looking straight into the eyes of Roger as he danced with Iris. She averted her face hurriedly. If she did not watch out, not only Roger, but the entire hospital, the whole world would know she was in love with him. Jerry spoke again.

"I suppose you think that because I said I wanted to get married—and to you, you think love means very little to men? If so, my dear Netta, you'd be wrong. But most men are more—what shall we say—philosophical about these things."

"What you really mean is, they don't feel so deeply. Isn't that it?"

"No, it is not," he said emphatically. Then he went on, in quieter tone: "It's silly to generalize of course, but on the whole women are tougher than men in the amount of pain and stress they can stand—mental and physical. Men therefore take steps, consciously or unconsciously, to avoid it, or get rid of it. See what I mean?"

"I think so. It's a sort of built-in security."

"In a way. But don't get the idea that men don't suffer. In their way, they suffer just as much as women do. Perhaps the difference between us is—knowing when to quit."

Knowing when to quit. "Is that what you did, Jerry? she asked quietly.

He pursed his lips. "Sort of. I wanted more from you than you wanted to give. Just friendship wasn't enough any more. So—what use to go on harping when it was plain you didn't feel the same? As I said, men know when to quit."

Men know when to quit. Netta thought this over quite a good deal during the days which followed.

How simple it sounded. And what exactly did it mean? Jerry had done it by simply telling her how he felt, then when he knew she did not feel the same way, putting an end to their relationship as it had been. What would quitting mean for her with regard to Roger? Stopping herself from thinking about him? Suppose he became engaged to Iris? Suppose they were married? She would have to take her feelings in hand then.

Easier said than done, she knew. At the present moment she didn't think she would ever stop loving him. She had never loved like this before. He was the one man in the world for her. But *was* he for her? Wasn't that wishful thinking?

Men knew when to quit. So did women, truth to tell, but they hung on to their pain like creatures in the power of a hypnotist. Or was it out of sheer self-will?

That weekend, Elva went home to see her parents. Netta had the flat to herself, and used her solitude to take a good long look at herself. She must make the effort to stop thinking about Roger, put him out of her mind. After all, she had worked alongside him for months before she fell in love with him. She could do so again. But if she failed in her resolve, then she would ask Matron to accept her resignation.

It cost her a great deal to make this decision, and tears gathered in her throat, but she denied herself even the luxury of shedding them. Instead, she got her car out of the garage and took herself for a run.

It was almost dusk when she set out. The countryside looked bare now. Autumn was nearly at an end, at times indistinguishable from winter. She tried to ignore the feeling of winter in her heart in a fierce concentration on her driving, watching the road surface, the oncoming traffic and that which showed in her mirror.

She felt her heart contract violently. The driver in the car behind her—it was Roger. Roger. And beside him was Iris. She glanced at the road ahead. All right, so it's Roger. You must expect this sort of thing, she told herself. This is the test. It was Sunday, and the day had been sunny. There was a good deal of traffic on the road. She tried to pull ahead, but he followed. Then she slowed down, hoping he would overtake her, but he couldn't. There were too many bends in the road, too much traffic both ways.

Flashing lights reminded her that it was time she switched on her own sidelights. Automatically, she glanced at her petrol gauge, and to her consternation the finger pointed EMPTY. Then she recovered herself. That had happened before and she had driven quite a number of miles afterwards. The gauge, it seemed, was not strictly accurate. But how long it had pointed to EMPTY she did not know. She began to worry. Where on this road was the nearest petrol station?

She glanced again in her mirror. She had lost Roger now. Either somebody had overtaken him or he had turned off. She didn't know whether to be glad or sorry. Had she not been so conscious of him behind her she might have glanced at the petrol gauge sooner.

Netta carried on for a few miles, then mercifully a petrol station came into view. She signalled and slowed down and turned off the road. She had pulled up in front of the petrol pump before she realized it was locked. She sighed and put the car into gear again. Traffic was streaming past. She caught a glimpse of Roger's car as she crawled towards the way out of the station. So he hadn't turned off, after all. She didn't think he had seen her. He was looking straight ahead. But it didn't matter; it mustn't. Iris had been laughing and talking, her head turned towards him.

Hundreds of cars passed, it seemed, before Netta could once more get on to the road. She drove at a modest rate, keeping her fingers crossed, metaphorically speaking, for her petrol to last until she came to a garage or petrol station which was open.

But it happened. Presently there was no response as she put her foot on the accelerator, the car gave a little grunt, then stopped. By now it was quite dark, and perversely the road seemed suddenly to have cleared of traffic. At the present moment there was not a car in sight. The road was empty as if the motor car had never been invented.

Netta spent a few minutes calming her own fears, calling herself names for being so irresponsible and stupid, and finally deciding that the only thing to do was stand in the road and ask the help of a passing motorist. But whether it was because of the dark coat she was wearing, car after car passed by without stopping. Then it began to rain, and soon it was pouring. She hurried back into the car and sat there for a while not knowing what to do next. The situation was beginning to look pretty desperate. Being a fairly new car owner, she was not used to this sort of thing. She had certainly never run out of petrol before, but then she hadn't really driven much of a distance on her own. There was nothing to driving to the hospital each day. She told herself ruefully that there was more in owning a car than the ability to drive.

She racked her brains. Should she sound her horn to try to attract the attention of a passing motorist? But that was against the law. Then she remembered how long-distance lorries signalled to each other. Perhaps she could do that—switch her lights on and off quickly. She did this next time a car approached, and to her relief it came to a stop on the opposite side of the road.

She got out of the car. It was still raining, giving the road a black, shiny appearance in the lights of the cars. She ran quickly across the road to the other car and the driver wound down the window. It was a middle-aged man and he was alone.

"Hello, hello," he said in a hearty voice. "What's the matter, then? Had a breakdown?"

She shook her head. "No,——" But she was interrupted.

"Good heavens, you're getting soaked! I'd no idea it was a young lady in trouble or I'd have got out myself." He opened the car door. "Look, get inside for a minute. I'll move over."

She protested faintly, but he insisted, so she slipped into his driving seat.

"Now then, my dear," he said in a fatherly fashion, "What's the trouble, eh?"

She told him. "I'm afraid I haven't even a spare can or anything. Could you stop at the next open petrol station or garage and ask them to bring some out to me?"

But he didn't hold out much hope. "Oh dear! It's Sunday, you know. Even the places that are open usually only have one man to operate them. But we'll fix up something for you, don't worry."

Netta began to feel uneasy. His tone of voice was altogether too soft, and he seemed in no hurry to help her.

"There are garages which run a breakdown service. Could you perhaps telephone one for me?"

"Yes, I could. But look, why don't you come along with me? We could go and have a drink somewhere. Your car will be perfectly all right here for a little while, and of course, I'd run you back."

Netta reached for the handle of the door. The sooner she was out of this man's company, the better. He might be harmless. On the other hand, he might not. But it was evident that he was more anxious for her company than to be of real assistance. It would be better if she had another try for help. The next motorist might not be alone and might be less forthcoming.

But to her consternation he tried to stop her opening the door.

## CHAPTER FIVE

NETTA struggled in vain. "I shall report you to the police," she gasped in desperation. "Let me go at once, I tell you!"

But still he held her. "Take it easy. I'm not going to hurt you," he said smoothly.

It was no use. Cars flashed past, and she wished one of them would stop. But why should they? She made a silent vow that never again would she allow herself to get into a situation like this.

The more she tried to free herself of the man's grasp the more firmly he held her. She was just wondering whether it might not be best if she pretended to relax, then perhaps he would be taken off his guard, and she could get free, when the figure of a man shining a torch loomed up beside the open window of the car. To her surprise a familiar voice sounded.

"Is that you, Netta? Are you all right?"

Unbelievably, it was Roger. Quickly, the man in the car released his hold on her, and Netta opened the door and stepped out on to the road.

"Roger! Oh, Roger, thank goodness you've come!"

His face looked black. "What's happening? Do you know this man? Has he been annoying you?"

But before she could answer, the man slammed the door sharply and pulled his self-starter.

"Just a minute——" Roger shone his torch on the round fat face.

"I was trying to help her, that's all, but she never gave me a chance," the man blustered. "If you're a friend of hers, I'll be on my way."

The next minute the car shot forward, and they had to step out of the way quickly to avoid being struck by the back wing.

The rain had now almost stopped. Roger grasped her by the upper arm and looked down at her.

"Roger, how——" she began, then halted at the taut expression on his face.

"If you didn't know him, how did you come to be in his car?" he demanded.

She stared at him. "I—I got in out of the rain."

"But why?"

She felt like a child whose actions were being questioned by its parent or teacher.

"I—I ran out of petrol. It took me ages to get anyone to stop. Then this one did, and I got out. It was pouring with rain."

His eyes took in the state of her hair. "You're wet through. Go and get in your own car. I've got a towrope in the boot of mine. There's a garage open in town. Wait!" he added sharply as a car rushed towards them, its headlights almost blinding them. "All right?" he asked after a second or two when they had recovered their sight. "Well, come along."

He conducted her to where her car was standing, his grasp still on her arm. She was a mixture of feelings. It seemed so natural, so right that he was here, so right that he should be taking charge of her. A small voice issued a warning, told her she shouldn't be indulging in such whimsies, however, and weak though the voice was, it was effective.

There were several things she wanted to ask him, but he bundled her into the driving seat of her car with little ceremony. His own car was on the other side of the road. He must have driven up quietly while she had been struggling to be free of that horrid man. He crossed over to it and drove it to just in front of hers. It was then that she saw the answer to one of her questions. Iris was sitting in the passenger seat. She turned and looked at Netta, but did not get out or even wave. Perhaps she was annoyed that Roger was doing this. How had he known she was stuck? That had been the other question she had wanted to ask him.

Roger got out the towrope and attached it to the rear of his car, and tied it firmly on to the fender of hers. That done he came to speak to her. She wound down the window.

"Now listen carefully, Netta," he said. "This is important. Your handbrake will be off when we get going, so you'll have to control your speed by means of your footbrake. Keep your foot lightly on it the whole time, increasing the pressure just sufficient to keep the towrope tight. Understand? If you don't do that you'll be in danger of colliding. Watch my brake lights carefully. If they come on, put yours on, but gently, not suddenly. I shall try to keep my speed to around a steady thirty. You'll have to watch out for what the other traffic might do as well. That way, you'll be able to anticipate my actions to some extent. I'll give you my signals in good time." He smiled suddenly. "Apart from all that, all you've got to do is steer. It's a tricky business being on tow, but I'm sure you'll manage. Leave the gear in neutral, of course, and drive with your headlights dipped, O.K.?"

"Yes—and thanks, Roger. I'm sorry I'm being such a nuisance."

He gave her a stern look. "I'll have a word to

say to you about that later. By the way, if you're in any difficulty, just sound your horn."

It was a little tricky, as he had said, and needed all her concentration to keep exactly the right distance from his car, but after a few miles she began to get used to it. Used to it enough to be aware of Iris's head close to his, to notice the number of times she turned her head to speak to him, to wish with all her heart that it was she who was sitting there beside him, indeed to feel her heart slowly being torn apart. By the time they reached the garage tears were mingling with the drips from her wet hair and quiet sobs were gathering in her throat.

At the garage, Roger got out of his car immediately and went to her.

"That was well done. How many gallons? Two do you for now? You don't have to get out. Stay where you are."

She said two would do, and he gave the order to the attendant. Then he came to the open window again.

"Are you all right, Netta? You still look pretty drenched and—rather pale. I'd suggest a hot bath and straight to bed with a drink."

She simply dared not look at him. She reached in her pocket for a handkerchief and blew her nose vigorously. Roger seemed worried. He put his head through the open window again.

"Would you like me to come—to see you home?"

Iris sat aloof in his car. Netta guessed she must be feeling annoyed that he had done what he had.

"No, no, Roger, I can manage now. Thanks very much indeed for all you've done."

Now he was looking angry. "Somebody should give you a good talking-to about how to run a car. You should be prepared for these emergencies. But I won't nag you now. Best thing you can do is get home and to bed just as quickly as you can. Just a second while I untie the towrope, then off you go."

With a sense of hopelessness she watched him untie the knots, then she started her engine and drove off slowly. She had just been a nuisance to him, that was all. She meant no more to him than just someone he knew and whom he had helped. She felt so miserable and unhappy she just wanted to die.

Almost the first person she saw the following morning was Iris, who said scathingly:

"You caused us a whole heap of trouble last night, didn't you? Fancy letting yourself run out of petrol. But what's more stupid—fancy getting into a strange man's car!"

Netta heaved a sigh. "I don't want a sermon from you, thanks Iris. I'm sorry if I inconvenienced you, but I dare say I would have got out of it somehow."

"Well, there's gratitude for you!"

"I'm grateful enough to—Mr. Henderson, and he knows it."

Iris gave her a look of scorn. "For your information, it was I who persuaded him to turn back. He was glad, afterwards, that I had, of course. But it was I who saw you at that petrol station, and——"

This was a further slap in the face, and Netta wondered, silently, whether there was to be any end to her suffering.

By lunchtime the whole hospital seemed to know that she had let herself run of petrol and had had to be towed to a garage. And from all quarters came good advice as to what she should do. Jerry and Hugh were both genuinely concerned, and almost throughout an entire operation for strangulated hernia told her what she should do in future.

"I always carry a spare gallon in the boot."

"Always look at the petrol gauge before you set out on any journey."

"Especially on Sundays."

"Do you belong to the A.A., Netta?"

"Or the R.A.C.?"

"You should always carry the handbook and key with you."

Roger kept silent for a while, then he said curtly. "You two are a little late with your advice, aren't you? After all, Sister's had her car for some months now."

Hugh and Jerry exchanged a glance. Then Hugh remarked: "Isn't that being 'wise after the event', too? I guess we took it for granted that a woman of Netta's intelligence would have joined a motoring association and so on."

"A person can be intelligent in one direction, and quite lost in another," Roger answered.

"Too true, and I blame myself entirely," Jerry put in. "I should have been the one to have seen to these things for her."

Netta listened to all this without saying anything. She wanted to ask them for goodness' sake to let the matter drop, but training kept her silent. Away from the operating table she would probably have rounded on them all. As it was, there was little she could say, except answer yes and no to their questions.

When the operation was over Roger spoke to her. "How are you feeling after your adventure?" She told him she was fine. Then he said with a slight smile, "I had intended to read the riot act to you, but I think you've had all the advice you need from the other two. You—will be careful in future, won't you?" he added.

And before she could answer him, he turned and went out swiftly. He had sounded concerned. But was he really? Was it true that it had been Iris who had persuaded him to turn back in case she was out of petrol?

It was Jerry who bought her a petrol can and filled it with petrol for emergencies, who saw to it that she joined both motoring organizations.

"That way, you have two lots of keys to the telephone boxes, and two chances of getting help from their road patrols in the daytime. I'm sorry, Netta, about what happened to you. But somehow it never crossed my mind that you'd be careering around on your own after dark. I somehow imagined you just used your car for short runs locally. Anyway, always carry the handbooks and keys, a large torch, a good map so that you can find out where the nearest garage or village is, and as you drive along, take notice, and memorize, the location of the A.A. and R.A.C. boxes. Above all, you must make arrangements to have your car serviced regularly. Understand?"

"Jerry—this is awfully sweet of you——"

"Nonsense," he said gruffly. "It's only what I should have done long ago."

Jerry had called to see one evening when Elva was still on duty. It was the first time she had been in his company alone since the night he had asked her to marry him.

"Are you—waiting until Elva gets in?" she asked him when they had exhausted the subject of her car.

He stretched out in an armchair, his long legs at right angles, and looked at her, an unusually gentle smile on his face.

"You know, I've missed you, Netta," he said, not answering her question.

"I've missed you, too, Jerry."

"But you've consoled yourself with Hugh."

"Oh, Hugh's all right. How are things with you and Elva?" she asked.

He shrugged. "All right, I guess. But habit dies hard. I'd got used to you."

"But you knew when to quit," she reminded him, but not without a sudden stab of pain as she thought of Roger.

"It hasn't been easy," he said quietly.

"I know."

She answered without thinking, and he sat up and stared at her.

"What's that supposed to mean?"

She shook her head vigorously. "Nothing, Jerry. Just that I—understand how you must have felt."

He subsided into his chair again and thrust both hands in his pockets.

"Lord, Netta, I'd give anything to have things different between us."

She stood up and went to the window. "Jerry, please don't.

It was doubly painful to hear him talk this way. Life was cruel at times. It seemed incredible that a short time ago she was so happy and carefree. Now she was having to hurt Jerry, and she herself was tormented at every turn by a love such as she had never known before, yet it was hopeless. She had never thought it possible to be so overwhelmed with a love like this. She felt Jerry's hand on her shoulder.

"Don't let it get you down, Netta," he said lightly. "It will all come right in the end, as they say."

"Oh, Jerry——"

In a sudden rush of emotion, of affection for him and in her own need, she turned to him. His arms came about her tightly for a moment and she clung to him. Elva chose that moment to fling open the door and stand staring at them in shocked surprise. For a moment Jerry did not move, then easily, his arms dropped to his sides.

"Hello, Elva. Don't mind Netta and me. It was just for old times' sake, that's all," he explained casually.

Elva appeared to recover. "Well, if you're sure——"

But Netta was not deceived. She could tell from Elva's manner as they all had tea together that she was more upset than she had admitted. And later that night as they prepared for bed, she said quietly:

"Jerry's still in love with you, isn't he, Netta?"

"Elva—please——" Netta protested. Then, relenting: "I'm sorry. But I don't know what the answer is. It takes time, you know. You can't expect him to—to change his feelings overnight."

"You're not giving him much chance, are you?"

Netta colored. "That's not fair! I'm not encouraging Jerry, if that's what you mean. He called to bring a can of petrol anl some forms for me to fill in to join the A.A. and the R.A.C. There was nothing to what you saw as you came in. Nothing at all."

"Maybe you didn't see the expression on Jerry's face."

Netta sighed. "Look Elva, I'm sorry if Jerry isn't coming up to expectations, but that's no fault of mine. Give him time and he'll get me out of his system—as far as I'm still in. It will all sort itself out," she finished, not very optimistically, but more or less echoing Jerry's words.

"That's what people always say who are not in love themselves," Elva said in a hollow voice.

Netta could make no possible answer to this. Though it was not spring, it was, it appeared, the season of being in love so far as the personnel of the Emergency and Casualty Centre were concerned. All at once everybody was at it, but with the wrong people. *Would* everything ever sort itself out? Perhaps it would for Elva, at any rate.

And for Jerry. They were already seeing quite a good deal of each other, and Jerry must like Elva a fair amount to ask her out as often as he did. Sooner or later his love for Netta herself would shrivel, become no more than a faded scar. And if Elva continued to love him, there was every chance that she would take Netta's place in his affections.

And her own love for Roger? Would that shrivel or fade, too, if it remained unreciprocated? And there did not seem the remotest possibility of it being so. Certainly, she could not go on like this. If she could not soon come to terms with the situation, she would simply have to leave the Centre and go somewhere else far away, abroad even. Yes, that was it. Why not? There were plenty of exciting and interesting looking posts offered overseas in the nursing papers.

The idea began to grow on her. She scanned the advertisements in the *Nursing Mirror* and the *Nursing Times* with a kind of determined enthusiasm.

She was doing this one day when Elva peered over her shoulder.

"Hello," Elva said, half-jokingly. "Going abroad?"

"I might."

"You're not serious?"

"I'm seriously toying with the idea, anyhow," said Netta. She hadn't intended discussing the matter, but it was difficult to hide things from the person with whom one lived—without telling lies.

Elva gave her a keen glance. "But why? I thought you were happy and settled at the Centre. You were at one time. So much so, I envied you."

"Yes, I know."

How long ago that seemed when she felt happy and on top of the world with absolutely no problems whatever.

"You haven't answered my question," prompted Elva.

But this was one question she could not truthfully answer. Nobody must know how she felt about Roger.

"About why I'm toying with the idea of applying for an overseas post? Oh, I don't know. I'm happy enough at the Centre." This was true as far as the work was concerned, anyway. "It's just that —well, I think it would be rather nice to see something of another country. After all, I've got no ties here."

Somehow, she made herself say the last sentence. She would have given anything for it not to be true.

"Your friendship with Hugh still platonic, then?" Elva queried.

"Yes."

"And what about your parents? Won't they mind your going abroad for a long period?"

Netta shook her head. "They won't mind. I can only get home during the holiday periods, anyway. And, bless their hearts, they are inclined to be absorbed in each other. Anyway, don't say anything about this, will you? I haven't really made up my mind yet, and I wouldn't like it to reach Matron's ears via the grapevine before I've been to her myself."

"Fair enough."

Deep down, Netta did not seriously think the time would come when she would actually go abroad to work, but reading the various advertisements, getting books out of the library and reading about the different countries one could go to gave her something to think about. The swimming pool at the Central Hospital in Salisbury, Rhodesia, for instance, looked very enticing. Theatre Sisters were required in Bahrain in the Arabian Gulf, which sounded exciting and mysterious.

There were vacancies in California, South Africa, New Zealand and Canada, opportunities in the Far East, the Bahamas and Australia. The choice was wide, and Netta worked hard at the business of pretending how interesting it would be to spend a year or two in these places. Painful thoughts of Roger, visualizing herself climbing into a plane and putting swift mile after mile between him and herself she tried to banish. There was no point dwelling on that aspect. Once or twice she asked herself if she were not going too much on assumption. Roger was probably not in love with Iris at all. Maybe she was just jumping to conclusions.

But each time she had any thoughts of that nature either something happened or someone said something which piled up the evidence more concretely. Iris herself would talk about where they had been, what they had done, Roger and she.

"Roger and I were looking at some contemporary furniture the other day," she announced in the Sisters' sitting room. Then added, for good measure: "We've discovered we both prefer simple designs."

Netta felt herself curl up. There was only Elva and herself in the room at that moment, so Iris could hardly have been merely showing off.

Not having the least idea how Netta felt about Roger, Elva asked: "Looking at furniture, eh? Have things got as far as that with you and our Mr. Henderson?"

"Oh yes. But we don't want it spread around until we're ready to announce something definite."

Roger, too, had hinted at something similar, according to Hugh. Hugh had taken Netta to the theatre one evening, and to her dismay Roger and Iris came in together and sat only a few rows in front of them. Netta said nothing. She did not want either to draw attention to them or to talk about them. But Hugh bent his head towards hers, saying:

"Look who's just come in—Iris Leighton and Henderson. They're always together these days. From various things he lets slip out, they'll be married before long. And I should think Iris'll be good for him."

"Do you think so?" Netta answered in a hollow voice.

But Hugh didn't really seem to hear her. He sat there smiling, watching the two as they settled in their seats. It was odd, but seeing them together appeared to please him enormously. Or was it only her imagination? Perhaps he was in a particularly good mood this evening. He was certainly more attentive, once he had finishel watching Roger and Iris, touching her hand, paying her compliments in a way he had never done before, and, in a way, it was soothing to Netta's wounds.

When the curtain came down on the first act, he suggested a drink in the theatre bar.

"Do you really want to go, Hugh?" she asked, wanting to avoid the possibility of coming face to face with Roger and Iris there.

Hugh looked at her and gave a smile which seemed to have a touch of humor.

"Don't you?" he queried. "Oh, come on, Netta. It'll do you good. I think you need cheering up. You haven't been looking too bright lately, anyhow."

He took her hand and stood up. A glance in the direction of Roger and Iris showed that they were still in their seats, so she rose and followed Hugh, stepping carefully over the feet of those still sitting down.

In the bar Hugh found a seat for her, then went to the already crowded serving counter. Netta glanced around the place at the variety of people who stood around and chatted. Normally, this gave her pleasure, to observe people, to wonder about them, to watch their faces as they talked, to try to guess what their relationship was, one to another. But being in love with Roger yet outside his life robbed her of the ability to enjoy things as she had formerly.

Then suddenly Roger stood before her, a look of surprise on his face.

"Hello, Netta," he said. "Not alone, are you?"

She shook her head, and Roger glanced around and caught sight of Hugh.

"Ah yes, I see—Raven. Will you excuse me, Netta? I must get a drink for Iris. She'll be along in a moment."

When Iris appeared, she, too, was surprised to see Netta. Evidently she and Roger had not seen Hugh and herself sitting behind them.

But her look of surprise soon changed to a supercilious smile.

"Well, hello! Fancy seeing you here. Have you seen Roger? Ah, there he is," she went on, catching sight of him.

Netta made room for her to sit down on the benchtype seat, but either Iris didn't see the gesture or ignored it. She strolled over to Roger, and as if wanting deliberately to wound Netta, put a hand possessively on his shoulder. He turned to her, his expression soft, and Netta wondered if there was any greater agony than this. She was about to get up and go, to the powder room, anywhere away from here. But Hugh turned from the counter with two drinks in his hands. He saw Roger, spoke to him, and gestured with his hand to where Netta was sitting.

A broad smile on his face—the smile, in fact, Netta thought, of any normal man enjoying a night out—Hugh came towards her.

"Phew, what a crush! Never saw anything like it. Hope this is all right for you."

If it had been the deadliest poison Netta would have said yes. What did a trivial thing like a drink matter?

"Thanks, Hugh," she said, and was amazed that she sounded quite normal.

Some people moved, and Hugh sat down. "Let's spread out," he said, "then the other two can come and sit with us."

Netta looked at him a little puzzled. "I thought you didn't like Roger Henderson?"

Hugh's face became a mask, his eyes expressionless. He didn't speak for a minute, then he took a drink and said with a slight lift of his shoulders:

"If I do, then it isn't merely prejudice, I assure you. I just heartily dislike some of the things he says—and does."

A little knot of pain robbed her of other kind of emotion. "I—don't understand, Hugh. What kind of things? He seems to me a—well, rather an admirable person."

Hugh gave a short laugh of derision. "That's the way he gets most women. Worshipping at his feet—until they find him out."

She began to dislike Hugh. "I'm sure that's not true. At any rate, I've seen no evidence of it among the nurses and Sisters."

"No? Look at Iris—and you."

She colored. "But that's nonsense. I'm not—worshipping at his feet, as you call it. As to Iris, she's probably genuinely in love with him—and he —he with her. You have absolutely no grounds at all for saying that's the way he gets most women—sort of hinting that he works at it deliberately."

Hugh raised his brows. "There you are, you see, rushing to his defence like a tiger defending her young."

She tried to fight down her anger. For one thing she dreaded really giving herself away, and for another, she was Hug's guest for the evening.

"But that still doesn't justify your saying that's the way he gets *most* women."

Hugh smiled grimly. "Ah! Give him time. He's only just started. He hasn't been here long enough. He's the kind that works slowly, pretends to be aloof, gets everybody wondering about him, women interested in him, then——" He broke off. "Ah, here comes Iris, and dear Roger just leaving the bar."

As Iris came towards them, Roger following with their drinks, Hugh rose and gestured to a seat. She sat down, but Roger said he preferred to stand.

"In that case, I'll stand, too," Hugh said. "It gives me a pain in the neck looking up at people. Of course, I wouldn't mind looking up at either of you two beautiful girls," he added, smiling from Netta to Iris.

Roger's face was unusually serious as he stood looking into his glass, then, as if feeling Netta's eyes on him, he shifted his gaze to meet hers for a moment. She tried to smile, but whether her lips actually moved or not she really couldn't have said.

"Are you enjoying the show?" he asked her politely.

She made an equally polite answer, passing back the query, then he said:

"Where are you sitting? I didn't know you were here until I saw you just now."

"Hugh and I saw you come in," she told him. "We're about half a dozen rows behind you."

"I see," he said gravely, as if she had just given him some vital information.

The curtain-up bell rang at that moment and Netta rose to her feet, her drink barely touched.

"There's no hurry," Hugh said. "Finish your drink."

But Netta felt that to drink any more would have choked her. The bar was emptying rapidly.

She put her half full glass down on the table, saying that she preferred to get back to her seat in good time.

But she only took in a bare fraction of what the show was about. It was a musical which had had a long run in London, but her eyes strayed constantly to where Roger was sitting, and her mind kept churning over and over again the things Hugh had said. Why had he spoken like that? On what grounds was his opinion based? As though he knew what she was thinking, Hugh supplied the answer during the second interval.

First he asked her whether she would like to go and have another drink, but Netta couldn't face a repetition of the first interval.

"You go, if you want to, Hugh," she told him. "I'll stay here."

But he shook his head. "No, I'll stay here with you." He looked to where Roger and Iris were sitting. "Doesn't look as if they're going, either. You know," he said, after a pause, "a friend of mine worked with Henderson at his last hospital. I gathered he was practically thrown out. Got himself quite a reputation with the women."

Netta gave him a shocked glance. "Hugh, that's a terrible thing to say. I'm sure it's not true."

"Isn't it? What makes you so sure? Are you falling for him yourself?"

"Of course not."

"Then why do you defend him so much?"

"I'd defend anybody whom I thought was being misjudged."

"Is he being misjudged?" Hugh queried, eyeing her keenly. "What about that night he took you outside at the dance? That wasn't the kind of thing a man in his position should do. And I'll bet a pound to a penny that he kissed you. Right?"

95

Netta felt herself coloring, and knew it was useless to deny Hugh's guess. Nevertheless, she felt she must.

"Of course he didn't. What do you think I am?"

But her denial did not deceive Hugh. He gave an amused smile.

"Your face has given you away, Netta. And you're still sticking up for him." He shook his head. "I tell you, that man has broken more hearts than he's done appendicectomies. And not only that, either. I could tell you a lot of things, but—well, there's such a thing as loyalty to the profession. I'm ony telling you these things now because I thought you ought to know. If I'd wanted to be vindictive or do him harm I could have done so by now."

The curtain went up on the final act, plunging Netta in the gloomy confusion of her thoughts. Why should Hugh want to lie? As he had rightly said, if he'd been merely wanting to be vindictive he could have talked about Roger to his colleagues before this. Tears pricked her eyes, and the lights and the colors on the stage angled sharply into each other. Why had he taken her out and kissed her that night? Obviously, he had no affection for her. She was a fool to have let herself fall in love with him. Yet how did one stop a thing like that? One cure, of course, was to fall in love with someone else. But this couldn't be done to order. Besides, her love for Roger was deep. This was no infatuation. She was no teenager to be falling in and out of love with every change of mood.

She looked down the rows of seats to where he was sitting. At the present moment she felt she would love him until the end of her days. This was love of the eternal kind. But could it be, if he were the type of man Hugh said he was, the type of man he appeared? Surely one fell in love with a person's character, which was bound up with personality.

Would she then wake up one morning to discover that her love was less than eternal, after all? A woman was capable of infatuation at any age.

Infatuation? She felt as if her heart would break.

## CHAPTER SIX

WHEN the curtain finally came down on the show, Netta tried not to look Roger's way, except to notice which entrance he and Iris were making for, then to join the stream of people heading for another. Hugh suggested supper at an adjoining restaurant, and as they entered, she glanced around, half expecting to see them there. But thankfully, they weren't.

Hugh did not mention Roger again, and she was thankful, too, for that. He kept up an amusing chatter, and she reflected on what good company he could be when he chose. She simply could not believe that he had been telling deliberate lies about Roger.

"Thank you so much for the evening, Hugh," she said warmly, when he pulled up his car outside the front of the house.

He turned and smiled at her. "It's been a pleasure. We must repeat it." He reached for her hand. "I've always liked you, Netta. You know that, don't you?"

She would have withdrawn her hand from under his, but it would have seemed small thanks for the evening. She wondered how to answer him, but couldn't think what to say.

He put his hand under her chin. "Mind if I kiss you?"

He didn't wait for her answer. He bent his head towards her and kissed her fully and long on the lips. Emotionally upset as she already was, her lips trembled, and she felt his kiss become more ardent, more demanding. Suddenly she found she was clinging to him, returning kiss for kiss, her emotions, her passion all mixed up with her love for Roger.

"Hugh—oh, Hugh——"

"Darling," he murmured, his lips close to her ear for a moment. "I had no idea you could be like this."

His lips sought hers once more, but now she was spent. "Hugh, please—I must go in now, if you don't mind."

With apparent reluctance, he let her go. "When am I going to see you again?" he murmured. "Tomorrow? Day after? It must be soon now."

She felt a little uneasy. What had she done? Had she given him the wrong impression of her feelings and stirred up his? But he had stirred something in her, too.

"The day after tomorrow. I'm off at five, and it's my day off the following day."

He kissed her hand. "Good. We'll do something special. 'Night, then. Pleasant dreams. Mine will be."

He didn't get out of the car, but simply opened the door for her from the inside. She ran swiftly up the path to the front door and let herself in. Was Hugh going to be the answer to her heartbreak for Roger? she wondered rather wearily as she climbed the stairs.

Always busy, the theatre was extra busy the following day, and Netta was glad of it. One Operation followed swiftly on another, most of them of a major kind, and calling for the skill of a variety of surgeons. Some were tragic, as in the case of the retired industrial worker who tried to commit suiside by jumping from a high building. His wife had recently died and his only daughter, devoted to her mother, had accused him of neglecting her. The element of truth this contained, coupled with his maladjustment to his retirement, had caused him to take this impulsive leap.

Though real enough to her, Netta's own problems appeared, for the time being, trivial, and became submerged as the nursing and surgical team worked on the man's injuries and talked sympathetically of the events in the patient's life which had led to his wanting to end it.

"Doesn't sound enough to warrant a suicide leap, all the same," Hugh commented from his place at the anaesthetic machine.

"Maybe not, viewed objectively," answered Stephen Monro, "but at sixty-five it can't be easy to come to terms with your conscience, live a lazy life when you've been used to a hard-working one, and be left without your life partner into the bargain. What do you think, Sister?" he appealed to Netta.

"I agree entirely. Everybody's problems are important to themselves. It's only other's people's problems which appear trivial."

"True, true," murmured Jerry, who was assisting. "The lover's leap isn't really funny any more than the old man's leap, and a teenager in love can suffer almost as much agony as a man waiting to be hanged."

But Hugh was in an argumentative mood. "I still think that if people faced life's ordinary problems as they came along, they'd be better able to cope with the big ones."

"All right in theory, dear boy," murmured Stephen, but a different kettle of fish in practice."

The patient had no sooner been wheeled out than Sister Jones thrust the notes of another one into Netta's hand. This time, it was a case for Roger—perforated gastric ulcer and peritonitis.

Working according to her rota, one of her staff nurses shoull have taken this, but it happened that Nurse Kelly had just gone off duty, and an operation of this kind required two scrubbed up nurses. Swiftly, the theatre was prepared and one by one the team assembled around the operating table. It was not until she handed Roger the first instrument, that Netta realized that, for the first time that day, Roger, Hugh and Jerry were all three together on an operation. The three people who, one way and another had played, and were playing, such an important role in her life.

She held out dissecting forceps and couldn't help thinking, briefly, of the knowledge Hugh had of Roger's past life. Was Roger unaware that Hugh knew these things about him?

Hugh had set up a blood transfusion for the patient and now sat on his stool, giving an eye to his flow-meter and watching the patient's pulse. Presently he began to whistle faintly, as he sometimes did when the anaesthetic was well under control. Then he began to talk, asking Jerry if he had seen the show he and Netta had seen the previous evening. Jerry answered briefly that he hadn't, and so Hugh went on to relate in detail what the show was about. Roger was separating the muscle layers. Jerry was busy with swabs and artery forceps, and both men concentrated on what they were doing. Every now and then Hugh paused for a reply, and Jerry made some brief comment. Roger said nothing. Netta wondered what he was thinking. This part of the operation was very much routine to an experienced surgeon and was bound to leave room for some thoughts not related to the job in hand.

"But, you know," Hugh was saying, "an evening like that depends largely on the company you're in for a real success."

"Naturally" Jerry said drily.

"Yes, it was a lucky day for me, Jerry, when you and Netta packed up."

Jerry made no reply. Roger had now reached the peritoneal layer, that fragile sheet of peritoneum.

"For God's sake, will you shut up?" he snapped suddenly.

There was a moment's sharp silence. Jerry glanced swiftly at Roger, and Netta caught a gleam of wicked amusement in Hugh's eyes as he said:

"Now, now, no need to lose your temper."

"Hugh, pipe down, will you?" Jerry said calmly. "Or if you must talk, talk about something less personal. I'm quite sure Netta doesn't appreciate being talked about in public."

"Quite right, Jerry, I don't. In any case, it makes concentration rather difficult."

"Well then, we'll talk about something else," Hugh said, unrepentantly. "We'll talk about a letter I had recently from a chap I know at Darley General."

Darley General. That was the hospital Roger came from. What was Hugh trying to do? This was unforgivable of him.

Roger froze for an instant. Then without looking up, he said harshly:

"Damn you, Raven, don't you ever stop talking?"

Netta handed him the sterily suction nozzle. Roger's concentration was unimpaired, but it was evident that the mention of his old hospital by Hugh had touched him on a raw spot. Would anything induce Hugh to hold his tongue?

Roger bent to his task and before Hugh could start talking again, Jerry began to talk, addressing his remarks solely to Roger. It was about some case, a previous one similar to the one on which they were operating. It didn't make a lot of sense, and was rather inconsequential, but Netta blessed him. Obviously, he was talking to stop Hugh from doing so. And it was the kind of talk that was in no way distracting or disturbing, the kind surgeons often engaged each other in and which made no difference whatever to the way they performed the operation.

When the operation was finished Roger left the patient to Jerry and walked out of the theatre without a word.

"And what in hell was all that about?" Jerry asked Hugh, as the theatre porter wheeled the patient through to Recovery.

Hugh laughed shortly. "It got him on the raw, didn't it just? I told you he was a dark horse."

"Just because he hasn't regaled all and sundry with details of his past? It can't be anything important, otherwise he wouldn't have got the job here."

"Important enough. A man's private life's his own to some extent, but there are some things that should be known."

"Such as?" queried Jerry.

"His dealings with the ladies, for one."

Jerry looked at him steadily. "Hugh, there are times when you make me positively ill. You're worse than some old woman."

"You wouldn't say that if a woman you were fond of was involved."

Jerry's glance sharpened. He glanced at Netta, then back to Hugh.

"Is that any of your business, Hugh?" he asked coldly.

"It could be, if you and I both happened to be— fond of the same person."

Jerry's light combination flashed on, and with a murmured: "See you, Netta," he went out.

With casual indifference Hugh gave his attention to his anaesthetic machine. Netta eyed him for a moment. She simply could not understand him. Why should he want to hurt Roger? It was nonsense to make believe he was protecting herself or Iris or anyone. She wouldn't have believed he was vindictive or spiteful. What then?

One thing was certain, Hugh's hints about Roger were piling on her own sense of hopelessness. He had simply been out for a cheap thrill, kissing her as he did. And because of it, she had fallen in love with him! It seemed preposterous. It just couldn't be the real thing. But her heartache was real enough, and she seemed unable to get free of it, except for short periods at a time, and even then, Roger was never far from her thoughts.

When Netta was getting into her car later to drive home to her flat, Jerry got into the seat beside her.

"Do you want a lift somewhere, Jerry?" she asked.

"No. I just want to talk to you. What was all that Hugh was blabbering about this afternoon in theatre?"

"I—really don't know."

"Oh, please, Netta, don't plead total ignorance. He's got something up his sleeve that involves you."

She heaved a sigh. "I don't know what gets into Hugh at times. He seems to know something about Roger. He has a friend at the Darley General."

"I gathered that much," Jerry said drily. "But what else? And how do you come in?"

"I don't, really. Hugh has some crazy notion that Roger tried to—sort of—well, you know——"

Jerry frowned. "Make a pass at you, work on your feelings?"

"Yes, something like that."

"Did he succeed?"

Netta closed her eyes. Why did everyone keep talking to her about Roger? *Why?*

"Oh, Jerry, please drop the subject," she said wearily. "I don't know what Hugh is driving at, really. I've had very little to do with Roger."

"Except that night at the dance."

"Except that night at the dance," she repeated patiently. "And all he did was take me outside for some air."

"All?" pursued Jerry. "Didn't he kiss you?"

"If you must know, Jerry, yes."

"I see," he said quietly. Then, after a moment's silence, "I remember now how starry-eyed you were afterwards." He turned to her, in a sort of exasperated concern. "Really, Netta, you don't mean to tell me you—you fell for him—just like that?"

Netta sat silent. Why was everyone and everything conspiring to pile on her agony? She would have to get away from here.

Jerry took her silence for admission. "I'll break every bone in his body," he muttered fiercely.

"Jerry——" His threat was vaguely comforting. "You know, it's high time you stopped worrying about me. I'm not worth it."

"That's what you think! I do worry about you. And if I thought either Henderson or anyone else was deliberately setting out to hurt you——"

"Roger Henderson has done no such thing, I'm sure. I don't know whether what Hugh says about him is true or not, but I'd certainly take it with a pinch of salt. It's very sweet of you, Jerry, to be so concerned about me, and I appreciate it. But you shouldn't, you know. There isn't a thing anyone can do about the way people feel. If there was, you and I would be planning our wedding by now."

He covered her hand with his. "I wish we were."

In a way, Netta wished it, too. If it were any use to wish that everything was as it was before that night at the dance, or that she and Jerry were back on their old relationship, and that time could be sent hurtling back to when she had been on top of the world with no cares, she would wish it. But those things only happened in fairy tales and pantomines or science-fiction stories. Would she, she wondered, have found love for Jerry enough to marry him, except for the way she felt about Roger? It was possible.

Then she thought suddenly of Elva. She was in love with Jerry. It would hardly be fair to her for Netta to encourage him in any way whatever.

"I'd better be off, Jerry, if you don't mind— unless you want to come along to see Elva."

But he shook his head. "I won't bother, thanks. It's been one hell of a day, and I'm not really fit company for anybody—except you."

He put out his hand to the handle of the door, then suddenly turned back to her, and before she realized his intention he pulled her towards him and kissed her fiercely, with more anger than tenderness. But with a muttered 'damn' he let her go, a rueful smile on his face.

"Sorry, Netta," he said, touching her face. "I shouldn't have done that. Forget it, eh?"

He said goodnight and got out of the car. Netta drove to the flat thinking about him, going over some of the times they had spent together and recent events. They had been good times. If only they could have remained friends as they once had been. But changes occurred in life, and one had to accept them. How slow people were, though, to accept change, if it were not what they wanted. Life would be so much easier, so much more simple if we *could* accept more readily the changes that time or circumstances or any other force imposed upon us, she thought sadly. For instance, why could she not just accept the fact that Roger did not love her? Was there something wrong with her? Ought she to be able to?

But Elva appeared to be suffering from the same malady. When Netta entered the flat, she was sitting near the window looking gloomily out. They exchanged a few remarks about the day's work and so on, then Elva said:

"By the way, you thought any more about getting that job overseas?"

Netta sighed. "Not seriously. I suppose I don't really want to go, at heart, and I'm hoping, in a vague sort of way, that——" She broke off, partly because she wasn't quite sure what she was hoping for, and partly because she suddenly realized that Elva knew nothing whatever of her feelings for Roger.

"What are you hoping for?" Elva queried.

"Oh, nothing——"

"That usually means something. But of course, if you'd rather not tell me——"

Netta gave a faintly humorous smile. "I suppose I might as well, then we can really go to town on comforting each other."

Elva stared at her. "What are you talking about? Do you mean——"

"I mean that it looks to me as if we're both in the same boat. You're in love with Jerry, aren't you? Well, I'm in love with somebody, too. Someone who—to all intents and purposes is in love with someone else."

Elva frowned. "Good lord!—Hugh?"

Netta shook her head. "No, not Hugh."

Roger's name stuck in her throat. She didn't want to talk about him somehow. But Elva made a guess.

"You don't mean—not Roger Henderson?"

"How did you guess?"

"Oh, I don't know. That night at the dance, I suppose, and the way you dry up when Iris talks about him, come to think of it." She was silent for a minute. "Poor you! I know how you feel exactly. And to think I almost hated you because Jerry couldn't seem to get you out of his system. That's why I was anxious for you to go abroad." She gave a brief laugh. "As a matter of fact, I was getting round to thinking I might go with you."

"Terrible, isn't it? Pity women can't join the French Foreign Legion."

They looked at each other wryly. "It's not funny, really, is it?" Elva said with a sigh.

Netta agreed that it wasn't. "But I wouldn't give up hope, if I were you. Jerry's a very warm-hearted person. He needs love, and he needs to express it. He'll turn to you before long, you'll see. I'm the one who should clear out."

"And leave the field clear for Iris?"

"But what's the use if he's really in love with her? I'm only making life miserable for myself by staying here. It's different for you. Jerry takes you out now and then, and he likes you already, whereas I might not exist so far as Roger is concerned."

"I don't think that's quite true," said Elva. "I admit Iris seems to have got her hooks into him, but who's to say how far she's exaggerating in some of the things she says about him."

"I might be prepared to believe that if she were the only one who talked of, or hinted at, their possible engagement. But she isn't."

"Why, who else does?"

"Hugh, for one. And I've seem them out together frequently myself. But let's talk about something else, Elva. I keep trying to get Roger out of my mind, but somehow everywhere I go and everyone I talk to seems bent on discussing Roger. It's fantastic."

"You wouldn't notice so much if you weren't in love with him," Elva pointed out. "You know, you've given me a bit of advice about Jerry. Let me give you some about Roger. I know you won't agree with this, but if I were you, I'd try to get him away from Iris. She's no good for him, I'm convinced. I don't know how she's managed to get as far with him as she has. I'm sure it's not by fair means. Now, if you were to——"

"Elva, I can't!"

"Too proud?"

"Maybe. After all, he sees me every day. If——"

"Look, men are invariably blind to the thing under their noses. He's too good for somebody like Iris."

Netta moved restlessly in her chair. "It's no use, Elva, I just can't—sort of push myself under his nose. You can't force love. I want a man who's willing to chase *me*, as it were. What kind of love is it that you've got to almost trick a man into?"

"Listen, Netta——" Elva was really warming up to her subject now. "You want Roger—or any man— to love you enough to want to come after you. But why? Just because you're a woman? Why shouldn't it be the other way round? Many a woman doesn't realize she *is* in love with a man until he begins to chase her, to put it crudely. Well, if *you're* the first to discover how you feel, why shouldn't you do the chasing? It's as simple as that."

"But it's *not* as simple as that," Netta argued. "For one thing, you're assuming that I'd only have to "chase" Roger for him to discover he's in love with *me*. He probably wouldn't at all, and I'd be left looking cheap, and even more miserable into the bargain. Besides, it's just one of those traditions that it's the man who does the chasing. I can't very well say to him: "Would you care to come out to dinner with me?"—now can I?"

"It's a very moot point whether the male *is* the chaser," Elva asserted. "Besides, you don't need to be quite so obvious. There are ways."

"All right, you tell me some," declared Netta, entirely unconvinced by Eva's arguments. "Anyhow, I haven't noticed you practising many wiles on Jerry."

"Ah, you haven't seen me. You don't know what goes on in the plaster room."

"No? Plenty of hard work and not much else, I suspect." Then, more for the sake of something to talk about than a genuine desire to know, she went on: "Well, go on, I'm waiting. Just tell me how in the world it's possible to make a man fall in love with you without really trying. Or at least, without seeming to be trying."

"Of course, I haven't succeeded myself yet," Elva pointed out. "But I have made some effort. Anyway, Netta, you know the kind of thing just as well as I do—being extra nice to him, letting him know you like him, going to the places he's likely to be."

"That only piles on the agony. It's just horrible seeing him with Iris."

"I didn't say where he's likely to be with Iris," Elva reminded her. "Anyway, there's one thing you could do—stop being seen with Hugh. Maybe Roger would like to ask you out, but first you and Jerry are inseparable, then you start seeing Hugh."

Netta shook her head. "Elva, this is just idle talk, and you know it." She thought of that night she had fallen in love with him. She had tried to be extra nice to him on that occasion, had even flirted with him a little. And what had happened? He had retaliated by flirting with her, too. With devastating results so far as she was concerned. To him, it had meant nothing. She was willing to believe Hugh that he was nothing more than a breaker of hearts. "It wouldn't make any difference if I did stop seeing Hugh. In any case, I've promised to see him tomorrow."

In actual fact, she was very grateful for Hugh. He had been a great comfort, a safety valve. The only thing for her to do was take herself in hand and forget Roger. If she couldn't do it by remaining here, she would just have to leave. The thought of carrying out Elva's suggestion of getting him away from Iris, whether made seriously or not, was repugnant to her.

But whatever one's private troubles, life had to be lived, one's job had to be done. Netta scrubbed up for two of Roger's operations the following day, a case of severe burns and an acute abdomen. She thought once or twice that he seemed to be under some kind of strain, and longed to ask him. In spite of all that Hugh had said about him she still felt concerned about him, still loved him.

He had no sooner finished his first operation—a case of internal injuries following a car accident—when his lights were flashed on, indicating that he was wanted urgently.

He pulled off his gown and mask and dropped them on to the operating table.

"Shall I find out what it is for you while you drink a cup of coffee?" she asked him. "You—look awfully tired."

He gave her a direct look which had in it a little surprise.

"That's very kind of you, but I'd better go. I'll come back for the coffee, if I can. I'm not really tired. At least, not more than ordinary."

This little bit of personal contact sent a warm glow radiating throughout every part of her. This was what it had been like when she had first fallen in love with him, this core of happiness dwelling in her heart. What had she been doing with it these past weeks? Fighting it, stifling it, drowning it in her own self-pity?

Sister Jones came in with a note regarding a case for the orthopaedic surgeon, and Netta set about preparing the theatre feeling a new person. Roger came back just as it was finished. Netta, it not being her turn to scrub, saw that the coffee in the surgeon's room was all right for him.

"Rather a puzzle coming next, Netta," he told her. "Acute abdominal pain, but no rigidity or localization. Been vomiting for the past twenty-four hours. He's already had his appendix out, so it can't be that. There's no history of gastric or duodenal ulcer, and no evidence of intestinal obstruction, either. His general health is good, heart sounds are O.K., and a straight X-ray showed nothing abnormal."

Netta handed him the sugar bowl. "Has he a temperature?"

"Hundred and one, and he's sweating profusely. Also a very small amount of blood-stained fluid was aspirated.

Netta gave a puzzled frown. "There certainly isn't much to go on, is there? Do you think—a foreign body embedded somewhere?"

It was really wonderful to be talking to him, even if it was only shop talk. They used to have these kind of little talks about the work at one time, but not lately. She realized this suddenly, and wondered why it was.

Roger sipped his coffee, and said, in answer to her question: "A foreign body is a possibility, of course. But he has no recollection of swallowing anything. Still, the only thing to do is a laparotomy. A person doesn't have acute abdominal pain for nothing." He finished his coffee in one swallow, and gave a small sigh of satisfaction. "Thanks for that, Netta. I needed it."

She smiled at him. Why should she hide her love? she thought suddenly. It was nothing to be ashamed of.

"I must look after you a little more than I have been doing," she smiled.

He stared at her, his eyes gradually widening. "Well now, that will be nice," he said slowly, the beginnings of a smile curving his mouth.

The way he looked, the way he spoke, caused her color to rise. She turned away in confusion.

"If you'll excuse me," she murmured, "I'll go and see about getting the theatre ready for your laparotimy."

She didn't know why he should have put her to confusion, unless—— But it wasn't true, she was sure of it. He wasn't the Casanova Hugh had made him out to be. Yet there had been something about his smile——

She was allowing Hugh to influence her against her better judgment, she knew that. But why Roger's slow smile? Was it one of amusement? And that look in his eyes. Too incredulous, too significant. But significant of what?

She took her wayward thoughts in hand. She had a job to do, and she mustn't let her imagination run away with her.

Within a very short time the theatre was ready. The patient was wheeled in, Hugh caring for the the man anaesthesia-wise. Netta prepped the skin, laid on the operating sheet and clipped towels into place. Then Roger came in, gowned, gloved and masked.

"Thank you, Sister. Mr. Somers will be here in a moment. He got held up." He glanced briefly at Hugh. "Everything all right at your end, doctor?"

Hugh's eyes sparked over his mask. "Yes, sir, Mr. Surgeon, everything's O.K."

Netta picked up a scalpel. Had there always been this underlying antagonism between Roger and

Hugh without her noticing? But it had been open lately. Surely she'd have noticed that before? Roger took the scalpel from her and made his incision, and she put swabs and artery forceps to hand. Jerry came in after a minute or so and began talking about the case he had just seen—another car accident, probably fatal.

"They're doing what they can for him in Resuscitation, but he's in a pretty bad way. Steve's with him now. He'll want the theatre when we've finished here, I expect," He looked up. "Netta, my girl, there's one thing I forgot to tell you. Get a safety strap fitted to that car of yours, if you haven't already got one. You haven't have you?"

"No, I haven't. I didn't think I needed one. I never drive more than fifty miles an hour."

"No matter. Get one, next time you're out. I'll be checking up on you to see if you've done as I've told you."

"Well, well," said Hugh with faint sarcasm. "What a thing it is to have somebody to tell you what to do!"

"It's a very good thing at times, I imagine," Roger said quietly, after a moment's silence. "Netta might have cause to thank Jerry one day for his concern—though one hopes she will never have occasion to."

"You can say that again," muttered Jerry.

Now, Roger was concentrating on his operation, exploring with gentle fingers to find out the cause of the patient's pain and high temperature.

"Pass me a scalpel, Sister, I'll do a resection, then we can see what's there. Looks like an abcess." He probed, then brought out a large fishbone around which the abcess had formed. "There you are, Netta. Your diagnosis was correct," he said to her.

She picked up the kidney dish and its contents and put it on the lower shelf of the suture trolley.

"Thanks, gentlemen—and Sister," Roger said as usual.

He received a glare from Hugh, and Netta distinctly heard his muttered: "Who the devil does he think he is?" as he wheeled out the anaesthetic trolley.

She glanced at Roger. Surely he had heard, too? He could hardly have failed to. But if he had, he gave no sign.

"I believe it's your day off tomorrow, Netta," he said, as he stripped off his operating regalia.

"That's right."

For a moment they were alone in the operating part of theatre. All around, voices could be heard —the nurses in the clearing-up room, Jerry talking to Elva outside the plaster room adjacent to theatre, and Hugh saying something to one of the staff nurses in the anaesthetic room. But they seemed all part of another world to Netta. In her world there was only Roger. Roger and herself.

"And what are you doing?" he asked.

Her heart began to beat like fury. She was sure he would hear it, see the pulse in her neck.

"I—don't know," she answered jerkily. "Nothing in particular, as far as I know at the moment."

He smiled, and there was a twinkling humor in his eyes. "Well then, what about having dinner with me?"

She hardly knew what to say for a moment. This was so utterly unexpected.

"Do—you really mean it?"

"But of course I mean it. Why shouldn't I? What you said this morning about looking after me a little more gave me encouragement—or should I say courage?"

She didn't quite understand him, but she told herself recklessly that she didn't care.

"All right, then. Thank you very much. Where shall we meet?"

114

"I'll call for you at your flat, if I may. Better than meeting in a public place. Six o'clock be all right?"

In a daze, she said that it would, then as a nurse came in to start mopping up, he said: "Thank you, Sister," and pushed his way through the swing doors.


CHAPTER SEVEN

HALF an hour later, Netta went off duty, still feeling dazed. She couldn't believe it. Why had he asked her, if he were so nearly engaged to Iris? It didn't make sense. Then she was brought back again to what Hugh had said of him. It all tied up. He was unfaithful. He set uot deliberately to hurt people, women in particular. He hadn't required either courage or encouragement. He had been laughing at her. But, somehow, she didn't care. She loved him. Instead of fighting it she would accept it. She would enjoy his company tomorrow evening. If it meant pain later, then it would have been worth it.

She heard a voice call her name just as she was getting in the car, and looked round to see Elva.

"Had you forgotten I was off, too?" she panted as she hurried up to the car.

"I'm sorry, Elva. Yes, I had, as a matter of fact. Hop in."

Elva slammed the car door and settled in as Netta went through the process of starting up.

"You're looking chirpy," she said, eyeing her. "Something happened?"

Netta grinned widely. "You won't believe this, but Roger has asked me out to dinner tomorrow evening."

"He's what? Lord! Iris isn't going to like that. And did you say you would? Or is that a silly question?"

"I'm an idiot, I suppose, but I did say yes. I just couldn't resist it."

"I can't say I blame you. But I wonder why?"

"Why he asked me, you mean, if he's supposed to be serious with Iris? That's what I've been asking myself."

"Maybe he's not as serious as she tries to make out."

"But he is, according to Hugh, too. And why should Hugh want to exaggerate or anything?"

"Search me. Mind you, I think Iris is on duty tomorrow evening. But even so——" Elva broke off. Then after a minute or two, she said tentatively: "You know, Netta, I heard something about Roger Henderson the other day. I realize how you feel about him, but I really do think you ought to know this, if you haven't heard it already."

Netta felt herself go rigid. "What have you heard, Elva? And who told you?"

"I forget who told me. But it appears our Roger isn't quite what he seems. He was something of a knock-out in his old hospital, so I understand."

"That's what I heard, too."

"Do you think there's anything in it?"

Netta sighed. "Sometimes I do and sometimes I don't. And at the present moment I simply don't care."

Elva put a sympathetic hand on her arm. "I know how you feel. At any rate, your eyes are sort of wide open, aren't they?"

Netta almost forgot that she had promised to see Hugh that evening, until Elva asked her later whether she was going out. On hearing with whom, Elva looked up from her chair with an amused smile.

"Going it, aren't you? You'll be acquiring a reputation yourself, if you go on like this. Some say, in fact, that you and Jerry will come together again sooner or later."

Now the smile had vanished from Elva's face, and Netta paused on her way to the bathroom.

"Don't pay any attention to that kind of gossip. I was just a habit with Jerry that he's finding hard to break. But he will. In fact, he almost has. So don't worry."

But as she dressed to go out, she couldn't help thinking of his concern for her in the theatre this afternoon regarding a safety strap for her car. Was it just the concern of friend for friend, or was Jerry still in love with her? She hoped it was the former, for Elva's sake.

Her thoughts switched to Hugh. She regretted, now, the way she had responded to his kisses the last time they had been out together. It had been silly of her to give way to her feelings like that, and she hoped it wouldn't make any difference between them. The last thing she had wanted was that their friendship should become an 'affair'. It was impossible in any case, feeling as she did about Roger.

But Hugh was in anything but a loving, or even flirting, mood this evening. He drove his car to the front of the house and waited for her to come down instead of coming up to the flat for her. When she got in the car beside him he barely offered a greeting. Then he said off-handedly:

"Well, where would you like to go?"

She looked at him in surprise. "I don't know. Whatever you have in mind will do."

He shrugged and started the car. "In that case, we'll go for a run, then call in somewhere for a bite and a drink."

"Yes, all right."

After a while, she asked him if there was anything wrong. He didn't answer immediately. He kept his gaze on the road, his expression taut.

Then he said: "If you must know, I've just had one heck of a row with Henderson, blast him."

Netta cringed inwardly. It was dreadful to have to listen to things like this being said of the man you loved. But some kind of a reply was expected of her.

"What about?" she asked woodenly.

"Ah!" he snorted derisively. "I won't bore you with the details. I never met a man so overbearing, so full of his own importance."

"And yet such a lady-killer?" she came back sharply, without thinking.

He gave her a swift, barbed glance. "Exactly," he ground out. "If some of you women could only see him when he's with his own sex——"

His tone of voice was almost insulting. Netta felt a rising anger.

"Hugh, if you're not in the mood for a pleasant evening, I think I'd rather turn around and go home again."

He grimaced. "I'm sorry. But as a matter of fact, it's partly on your account that we had the row."

"On my account?" she repeated in astonishment.

Hugh nodded. "He was boasting that he had a tête-à-tête with you today. He thinks he's doing fine."

Netta shook her head in bewilderment: "I—I simply can't believe it," she said slowly, her voice little more than a whisper.

"I knew you wouldn't," Hugh said. "That's the damnable thing about it. You'd think butter wouldn't melt in his mouth. But haven't you got eyes, Netta? Or ears?"

She didn't know what he meant. All she knew was that she didn't want to listen to Hugh any more.

"Yes, Hugh, I have. But it's obvious they don't see or hear the same kind of things that you do. All you say may be true, but if you don't mind, I don't want to discuss him or listen to you running him down."

Hugh's lips and jaw became tight. She could only guess at what must be going through his mind. He drove in silence for a mile or two until the twilight deepened into gloom, then he switched on his sidelights. She did not know what he would say if she told him she was having dinner with Roger tomorrow evening. But there was no reason why she should tell him, and so she didn't.

Soon headlights were necessary, and Netta began to wonder where they were.

"Getting hungry?" Hugh asked her, seemingly in a better frame of mind.

"Not particularly, but let's not travel too far. We've got to get back tonight, remember."

"Have we?"

"Don't be silly, Hugh. Of course we have."

"I was only joking," he said. Are you still annoyed with me?"

"No, just a little ragged, I suppose."

"You'll feel better with something to eat inside you. I'll stop at the next hotel we come to."

Netta thought this sounded awfully vague, but said nothing until suddenly she noticed the petrol gauge.

"Good heavens, Hugh, you're nearly out of petrol."

He glanced down. "I'll get some at the next garage. There's bound to be one along here."

Netta remembered vividly the night she had run out. "But how do you know they'll be open, even if

119

there is one! We seem to be miles out in the country."

"For goodness' sake, Netta, stop worrying. Look," he said, as some lights appeared in the distance, "that looks like a hotel. I knew there was one somewhere along here. I'm not lost, if you are," he added with a touch of humor. "We'll go inside and get something to eat, and worry about petrol later."

She felt like saying that it might be too late to worry about petrol later, but thought better of it, if they were not to spend the whole evening in argument. Nevertheless, she felt uneasy, and decided privately that, no matter whose car she was in, in the future, she would check up on the petrol before setting out.

What Hugh said was a hotel actually was. He pulled into its parking area and led her inside the place.

"Now then, how about this, eh? For your information, we're only a few miles out of Dearing, and there's bound to be an all-night garage there, so we're all right."

The hotel was bright and modern, and they were served a very good meal. Hugh appeared to have shaken off his dark mood entirely, laughing and talking as he ate, and pressing her to finish the bottle of wine he had ordered. But Netta's mood had not changed. She was still uneasy, and wished he would get on with his meal and not talk so much. Even when they'd finished he still lingered, smoking a cigar and talking to the waiter.

She glanced at her watch and saw that it was nearly eight o'clock. Somehow she had not much faith in Hugh's talk of an all-night garage, and felt they should have gone in search of petrol first and eaten afterwards.

"Darling, what on earth are you worrying about?" he said, when she reminded him of the time. "We're too late for the eight o'clock garages, anyway, so what does it matter? Relax."

But her fears turned out to well founded. On checking up with the A.A. book, there was no all-night garage for another twenty miles. Netta was dismayed.

"Oh, *Hugh*, what on earth are we going to do now? We can't possibly risk running out of petrol on the road."

"You're right there, anyhow," he said easily. "We can put up here for the night. What could be more convenient? Come morning I can—I mean, we can——"

"But I don't want to stay the night here!"

"I'm afraid, darling, there's no choice. Sorry, and all that. In any case, I still can't see what you're worried about. It's your day off tomorrow, isn't it? You can ring the flat and let Elva know you won't be back tonight, and I can ring the hospital and say I'll be in in the morning as soon as I can. It's as simple as that."

Netta said no more, but she was angry all the same. Not because he had allowed himself to run out of petrol. That could happen to anyone, she supposed, as it had to herself. It was his whole casual attitude which angered her.

He went to ring the hospital—having fixed with the hotel proprietor for their overnight stay—and came back, a gleam of wicked amusement in his eyes.

"Guess who answered the phone," he chuckeld. "Our Mr. Henderson himself. He sounded quite shocked."

Before he had finished speaking, Netta had known what he was going to say. At this moment, she felt she hated him. A wild thought came that he had done this purposely. Yet why should he? He didn't know how she felt about Roger, and in any case, why should Roger mind what she did?

There seemed no motive for Hugh to have run out of petrol and suggested their staying the night here. She was letting her imagination run away with her again.

"What did you say to him?" she asked.

"Oh, just that we'd had a breakdown."

"Why did you mention my name? As you said, I'm not due at the hospital until the day after tomorrow."

"My dear, I didn't have to. He knew you were with me," he said smoothly.

"How did he know? Did you tell him?"

"Don't ask me how he knew. I didn't tell him. But why the terrific concern? Why all the questions? You don't let him worry you, do you?"

"You said he sounded 'quite shocked'," she pointed out. "I don't want *anyone* to be shocked on my account. There's nothing to be shocked about."

"Exactly. It just shows what kind of mind he has."

At this, Netta made a decision. She would not see Hugh again. She could not bear these things he said about Roger, not any more. Whether they were true or not was beside the point. Making the excuse that she wanted to freshen up, she asked for her key at the desk and went upstairs to her room. She stayed there for as long as she could without inviting comment, then went downstairs again. Hugh was chatting with a man at the bar, and as the hotel was not busy, Netta began a conversation, too, with the proprietor's wife. And so the rest of the evening passed without any further unpleasant comments, either about Roger or anything else.

Netta invariably slept badly in a strange bed, and so she was awake early the following morning. She lay awake for a while, then went along to the bathroom. It was a fine morning, and she opened the window and looked out. She could just see

Hugh's car. The hotel proprietor had said there was a petrol station about two hundred yards further along the road, so even if Hugh's petrol wouldn't get them that far, it wouldn't be far to walk for a can.

She was about to close the window when to her surprise Hugh appeared. She was puzzled. She wouldn't have thought he was such an early riser. Breakfast wasn't for over another hour. He went to the boot, and took out a petrol can. But why? she wondered. It was much too early to go to the petrol station. It wouldn't be open yet. But to her astonishment, he unscrewed the cap of the car's tank and proceeded to pour into it the contents of the can.

So he had had a gallon of petrol in the boot all the time! Surely he hadn't simply forgotten it? Yet what other explanation could there be?

Puzzled, she carried on with her toilet.

She was half way through her breakfast when Hugh came down. He said good morning brightly and joined her. She waited for him to tell her about the can of petrol, but he didn't.

After a while, she said: "Well, Hugh, do you think we shall manage to get to the petrol station on what was left in the tank last night?"

"Oh, possibly. In any case, it's not far to walk. By the way, I understand they close at six each evening, so we wouldn't have been able to get any from there last night. It's a lock-up place, too. Nobody on the premises, so we wouldn't even have been able to knock anyone up."

"You have your own can, then?"

He poured out coffee for himself, nodding. "I usually carry a spare gallon, but——"

"But this time you hadn't any in."

"That's right, sweetheart," he lied.

She was silent for a moment, then she said quietly: "It might interest you to know, Hugh, that I happened to see you pouring some into the tank this morning."

He started. "You did? I forgot to tell you. A chap I was talking to in the bar last night let me have a gallon from his tank."

She eyed him steadily across the table. "I saw you get it out of your boot."

He stared at her for a minute. "Did you get up at crack of dawn to check up on my movements? He gave it to me last night, of course. What are you trying to do? Make me out a liar?"

"No. You're making yourself sound like one. Why didn't you tell me last night, if it was so, or at least tell me just now when I asked you if we could get to the petrol station with what you had left in the tank?"

"Good grief, what is this?" he exploded, after a short silence. "I didn't tell you last night because you shot off to bed so quickly, and you've hardly given me chance to tell you this morning. You've been too busy shooting one question after another at me. All right, so I forgot I had the gallon in the boot. Now are you satisfied?"

It was Netta's turn to stare, and she had a sudden brief vision of what it would be like to be married to a man like Hugh. He was certainly a man with a very short temper. But she stood her ground.

"I thought you said a man in the bar gave it to you?" she asked.

"You've got me so mixed up, I don't know what I'm saying!" he almost shouted. He pushed back his chair. "Best thing I can do is get you back to your flat just as soon as possible. I'll have breakfast at a restaurant or somewhere. I'll pay off the manager and wait for you in the car."

He stalked out of the dining room. Fortunately, they were the only people in the room, otherwise the scene could have been most embarrassing.

124

Whichever way it was, Hugh had certainly lied, but somehow it no longer mattered what the truth was or why he should either lie or want to keep her here. She left the rest of her breakfast unfinished and went out to the car where Hugh was waiting bad-temperedly at the wheel. He started the car and drove to the petrol station without a word.

He kept up his silence until they reached the outskirts of Witteringham, then he appeared to relax.

"Well, here you are, safe and sound, neither abducted, seduced, nor yet made away with."

"I didn't expect to be any of those things," she answered mildly.

She wanted to add that, that wasn't the point. She just hated being lied to and being forced into a night in a hotel, willy-nilly. But she didn't want to start another argument.

He brought the car to a stop outside the house, and she thanked him, then reached for the handle of the door.

"You're in a hurry, aren't you?" he said.

"I should have thought you would be, too. In fact, you'll still be in time for some breakfast if you go straight back to the hospital now."

"Hm! No comment. What are you doing with yourself tonight? Shall I see you later on? No chance of being invited up now to have breakfast with you, I suppose?" he added, in a wheedling tone of voice.

"Sorry, Hugh, no," she said firmly. "And I'm afraid I won't be seeing you tonight. I have another engagement."

He pulled a face. "I see. Is that the truth, or are you still annoyed with me?"

"Of course it's the truth."

"Then what about your next evening? We'll do something definite, a show or dancing. And I promise I won't run out of petrol," he added, grinning.

Netta took a deep breath. "I'm sorry, Hugh. I'd rather not see you again."

"Eh? Oh, come now. You're not holding what happened last night against me, are you?"

"I've told you—no. At least, not as far as the petrol business is concerned."

"What then?" he demanded.

She opened the door. "Hugh, I don't really owe you any explanation whatever. I've enjoyed going out with you, and it's been nice of you to ask me, but I'd rather you didn't ask me again, that's all."

"All right, I won't, don't worry," he said in an angry voice, and almost before she had stepped on to the pavement he had started up the car with an angry roar.

Not feeling very happy, Netta mounted the stairs to her flat. Hugh had turned out to be a thoroughly unpleasant person. She could have put him off, she supposed, made excuses, but he would have had to realize it sooner or later. It was more honest to have told him plainly.

She spent the day doing odd jobs around the flat and shopping, thinking of Roger, looking forward eagerly to the evening with him. She was ready much too early, and the nearer the fingers of the clock drew to the time when he would call, the more her heart began to beat audibly. Was she dressed all right? she asked herself. Would he like her in the black velvet dress she was wearing? She had brushed her fair hair until her arms had ached, and fretted that it really needed cutting.

"For heaven's sake—you look fine," Elva assured her, laughing. "He isn't a duke falling for a duchess, you know."

*No, he's not a duke*, she answered silently. *He's a prince. And waiting for him, I feel like a princess.*

126

He was a few minutes late, and she began to panic. Suppose he wasn't coming? Suppose he had changed his mind? Suppose Hugh had told him—— But at last, from her post by the window, Elva reported that his car was drawing up, and Netta waited until he rang the bell, then went downstairs, feeling like a schoolgirl going out on her first big date.

"Will you come up for a few minutes?" she asked him.

He looked at her, smiling. "You look very nice," he said, his eyes flicking over her face and hair. "What a pity your hair is hidden for most of the time under a cap."

Her nervousness vanished, and she felt suddenly gay. "Well, that's a promising start to the evening," she laughed, leading the way upstairs. "Just keep on paying me those kind of compliments, and——"

"And what?"

"Never mind."

He looked round the room appreciatively. "So this is where you live, sleep and have your being. Very nice, too," he said, after he had greeted Elva. "You must come up to my sitting room some time. I understand it's allowed now and then, though what 'now and then' constitutes, I'm not sure. Just as long as the place isn't turned into a harem, I suppose."

Netta wondered whether Iris had ever been invited to his rooms, and tried to imagine the kind of belongings with which he would surround himself.

She asked him if he'd like a drink before they went out. "Sherry's all we have, though, I'm afraid," she added.

His eyes wrinkled in a smile. "Don't worry—if it's all right with you, I'd rather just go."

That suited Netta, too, so they said goodbye to Elva and went out.

This evening with Roger was something Netta felt she would never forget. So many things she saw him doing for the first time, so many things to learn about him. His hands on the wheel of his car, strong and sure. His eyes, seen so often above a gauze mask, now concentrating on the road ahead; his mouth, so often hidden, looked composed into easy lines. She sat well back in the passenger seat so that she could see his profile, and a wave of happiness washed over her just to be near him.

He did not speak for a little while, then he said: "That's only a bed-sitting room you have, isn't it?"

"Yes."

"It's nice and big, of course, but sharing it with someone else as you are—even if you get on very well together, which I expect you do—don't you ever want—even long for—a little real privacy? Aren't there times when you want to be alone, when you just want to sit and think your own thoughts without someone intruding into them all the time?"

Netta thought for a moment, going over her differing moods and phases of the past weeks.

"There *are* times when one longs for more privacy, of course," she said slowly. "But I'm not so sure that it's good for a person to be too much alone."

"Not too much, I agree. I know living alone can be pretty deadly, but of the two evils, I think I'd prefer living alone to living with the wrong person. One can always go out and seek company, whereas it'd be frustrating if you wanted to relax in your own place and give your mind to something, only to find you couldn't, and it was an inconvenient time to go and find a bench in the park."

Netta laughed. "A bench in the park has its limitations. You can usually get in, after dark, and if you tried sitting on a bench anywhere else at a queer time, you'd stand a chance of being moved on or even run in."

"Exactly. Not to mention the fact that it might be pouring with rain. No, I'd much prefer living alone."

Netta wondered why. There must be some other reason other than the ones he had spoken of. Usually, people hated living alone. It was only the thinkers, the dreamers who resented the intrusion of another human being. Even the artists, the selfish or completely egotistical needed an audience, people around them. Was Roger, then, a thinker? It would seem so from what he had said. What kind of things did he think about? she wondered.

"I suppose," she said, "It would be all right if *two* people who were thinkers were to live together. But even then, there'd be times when you needed to give your brains a rest."

He laughed. "How right you are!" Then, more seriously: "As a matter of fact, anyone who likes to be quiet, to think or read a lot, or write, would need to be very close to a person to live with them happily. And as a rule, that means a happy and successful marriage. Marriage with the right person, in other words."

Was he speaking generally or personally? She fell silent, day-dreaming, picturing herself as his wife. seeing him in an armchair by the fire, his head resting back, as he sat deep in thought. She woud sit there quietly with her knitting or sewing. She wouldn't disturb his thoughts. She would wait. And presently he would look across at her and talk to her, perhaps tell her what he had been thinking.

"A penny for them, Netta," he said. "Or am *I* the intruder into *your* private thoughts?"

How she kept from blushing she didn't know. She gave a light laugh. "Oh, my mind was just wandering," she said evasively. "You know, half the time when people appear to be thinking deep and fundamental thoughts, they're doing no such thing. There minds are a blank—if anyone's mind can be really blank—or else they're not thinking of anything in particular.'

He agreed. "Even so, it's nice and relaxing to let your mind just wander sometimes. But if you live with the wrong person, you might not even be able to do that in peace."

"But you have to give to other people sometimes," Netta protested, "and not just be content always to be sufficient unto yourself."

He agreed with that too, as she would have expected him to, and added:

"It's a case of mutual understanding and give and take, naturally. But that isn't always as simple as it sounds. People differ in their idea of what constitutes 'give and take'."

Netta laughed. "Ten per cent give and ninety per cent take, eh?"

"Exactly. Selfishness is something human beings have to fight in themselves continually."

This profound statement of Roger's brought them to the hotel where he had ordered dinner. It was one of those expensive places she and Jerry had never gone into. Netta politely made no comment, keeping to herself thoughts like—can he afford it? Is he out to make an impression or is this his normal standard?

He led her inside the thickly carpeted foyer, and after giving up their outdoor clothes, they sat before a huge log fire and drank an aperitif. Netta felt relaxed and happy. She had enjoyed their conversation in the car. She reflected with a little amusement that Roger might value his peace in which to think or let his mind wander, but he was also a good conversationalist, and liked to talk.

She looked at him to find that his eyes were upon her. He smiled.

"You look pleased about something. Is it the fire, the drink—or dare I hope, my company?"

She laughed. "Let's say it's your company. As a matter of fact, I was just thinking how funny it was that we talked almost without ceasing all the way down here, about the value of being able to be silent."

His smile deepened, and his eyes looked into hers in a way which made her almost panic.

"So we did," he said. "But I found the talk most interesting." He stretched out his legs and looked pensively into the fire.

Netta studied his profile for a minute, then gazed into the blazing fire herself, allowing her mind to indulge in fantasy again. This was their own hearth, just he and she in their own private, domestic world. They had no need of words. They were held in that pleasant state of contentment when the body, mind and even the spirit is at rest.

But soon Roger stirred, as if his thoughts were anything but pleasant.

"Comfortable here, isn't it?" she remarked.

"Not so bad," he answered. "Would you like another drink, or shall we go in to dinner?"

"Nothing more to drink, thanks," she said, and so they went into the restaurant.

As it was the season for game they ordered pheasant for the main course, and Roger chose a rich Burgundy.

"Do you often come here?" Netta asked him, as they began on the first course of Consommé Julienne.

"No, not often," he said briefly.

Netta thought he seemed to have become a little withdrawn, and wondered why. She concentrated

131

on her soup, but with the serving of the pheasant and the pouring of the wine he brightened again, as if remembering his duty as host.

He smiled at her across the table, and Netta was discovering that his smile did something to her.

"You like this place, then, Netta?"

She nodded. "I think it's absolutely wonderful, really. So comfortable, and at the same time having a touch of elegance."

"A good meal in good company and in pleasant surroundings takes some beating. Eating out is one of the necessities of life, but you might as well make it a pleasure and not just something to be rushed over."

"Which it is in hospital, more often than not. It's a wonder we haven't all got peptic ulcers. We rush at our meals even when we don't have to."

"Yes, life does tend to be all gulp and go," he said absently. Then: "Do you—er—ever long for a different kind of life, Netta?"

She gave him a puzzled look. "I'm not sure what you mean. Another kind of job altogether? Or marriage?"

"Well—either. Take the first one first."

She shook her head, and wondered what had prompted the question. Did he mean that he would like another kind of job himself?

"I—don't think I could imagine myself doing anything else except nursing," she said.

"No? But, Netta, what you're doing now isn't exactly nursing, is it? I mean, not in the traditional sense. Some women are so dedicated, as it were, they wouldn't be anywhere else but at the bedside."

She didn't answer for a minute. She wasn't sure that she quite liked the things he had said. True, she wasn't at the patients' bedside, but she still thought of herself as a nurse, not a theatre technician. What was he getting at? Was he hinting that, preferring theatre work as she did, she was not a true nurse?

He was smiling gently across the table. "I seem to have given you something to think about."

"Yes, you have," she said thoughtfully. "You may be right, actually. Thinking back, I really drifted into being a theatre nurse. What I mean is, I didn't start out my nursing training with the idea of working in an operating theatre. Most of the nurses in the same P.T.S. as myself had ideas of what they wanted to do once they were trained, but all I knew was that I wanted to be a nurse. Yet when I did do my stint in theatre I discoverel I liked it."

"And that you had an aptitude for it?"

"I suppose so. But I think what I liked—and what I like now—is the excitement of theatre, the drama."

"Ah, the drama. I'm glad you see it that way."

"Are you? Why?" she asked.

"Well, I see drama in things myself. You know, what you've just said is very interesting. In a way, you drifted into theatre work, and yet you're good at it."

Her heart gave a small leap of pleasure at his praise. "I hope so," she said modestly.

"You can take it from me, you are, and I'm not the only one who thinks so, either. But what I'm getting at is this: a person doesn't have to be dedicated in the traditional sense to be good at what they're doing. Few people are *truly* dedicated. And I'm not sure that it's a good thing to be. What's more essential, to my way of thinking, is to have enough of the right qualities to be good at whatever you turn your hand to. There's an awful lot of nonsense talked about being 'dedicated'."

Though she was sure he was right, it was rather shattering, in a way. 'Dedicated' was not a word

133

she would have used in speaking of herself, naturally. At the same time, one liked to feel that one was in the right job, that one was a true nurse without putting it into words.

"But surely, Roger, one has to feel that one is in the right job?"

"Yes, in a way. But for some people there may be more than one 'right job'. You can be good at more than one thing. You can have the kind of nature or character, the potential, which will fit you equally well for several jobs."

"Then you—don't consider yourself a dedicated surgeon?"

He shook his head slowly. "Not necessarily." He watched her expression, and she knew she must have shown her surprise, disappointment even. "Does that shock you?" he asked.

"I—I don't know. I suppose it does, really."

He shook his head in a different way. "It shouldn't, you know. Who's to tell that my experience as a surgeon—and even your experience as a nurse, though you may not know it—is actually a training ground for something else."

"But what else? I don't understand."

"Mine for another career, perhaps. Yours for—marriage. Who knows?" he said mildly.

She stared at him. "Do you mean you—you might give up being a surgeon?" she asked incredulously.

He eyed her quizzically. "Why? Do you think that would be wrong of me?"

"Well, I—it seems incredible to me that you should even contemplate such a thing. You're such a *good* surgeon. I simply couldn't visualize you doing anything else."

He gave a mocking bow. "Thank you. For the compliment, I mean. But don't you think that you couldn't visualize me doing anything else because you've never *seen* me doing anything else?"

"I—suppose so. But—but, Roger, good surgeons are not born every day."

"Good surgeons, like good carpenters, are made, not born," he corrected her. Then he smiled suddenly. "Don't look so shocked. I won't desert my post or anything like that. But you must admit it makes a good talking point. One thing is sure, I would never give up my surgery for any trivial reason. I'd have to be convinced it was the right thing to do."

"But, Roger, I don't understand why you should even be *talking* like this," she protested.

"Still shocked?" he said gently. "You shouldn't be, you know. Take the case of a woman surgeon. If she met a man and fell deeply in love with him, and married him, and had children, would she hesitate about giving up her job as a surgeon for another—that of caring for her children?"

"But that's different. If a man could easily give up a job like surgery for something else, then he shouldn't have been in the job in the first place."

"Why not? Especially if, while he *was* in the job, he was good at it." Then he laughed suddenly. "Poor you. I'm shattering your ideals, aren't I? But you know, some ideals are not really your own. They've been handed down to you, passed on by others via books and films. There is no reason at all why a surgeon should be put on such a pedestal. Yes, yes, I know he's saving life, and that's considered the absolute citadel. But there are plenty of other people whose job is saving life. There are many others, too, who are engaged in the business of making people's life *happier*. That, too, is important."

"The parsons and psychiatrists, you mean?"

"Yes, and others. Welfare workers, marriage guidance counsellors and so on."

"Well, to my mind, they're on a par with surgeons—I think."

"Ah!" Roger pounced on her last two words triumphantly. "Now you're beginning to doubt it. And when you begin to doubt things, you begin to think. If a surgeon, or a parson, or a welfare worker begins to feel either gradually or suddenly that he should change his job, that's not say he shouldn't have been in it in the first place, or that he was bad at it."

Netta gave in. "All right, all right, Roger. You have a point. I guess it's hardly fair to put anyone on a pedestal or to consider one job any more important than another—within certain limits, of course."

But Roger wouldn't even allow her limits. "I'd go further than the surgeons and parsons. What about the ordinary laborer? The bricklayers and—as I mentioned before—the carpenters? All these jobs have to be done. We have to have houses, furniture. Somebody has to build the surgeon's theatre, the hospital, the bed he lies on, the table from which he eats. Their job is just as important. It's different, that's all."

He had certainly given her something to think about. She wasn't convinced, by any means, that a bricklayer's job was as important as that of a surgeon, but she could see what he meant, and in a way he was right. Each individual, no matter what his or her pob, was equally important in his own right, and as a person. But Roger had a point of view she had never heard anybody else put forward. Never. In having these views he was bringing himself and his own job down to the level of that of everyone else. This made him a very humble, and a very unselfish person, a very different picture indeed from the one Hugh had painted of him. It was wonderful to be getting to know him like this, and the more she came to know him, the more she loved and admired him.

During the sweet course, he talked about books, and she discovered that his reading taste was wide, ranging from biography and travel to popular fiction.

"So that's what you do with all the time you spend alone in your rooms?" she said teasingly.

Too late, she realized she was saying the wrong thing, as a small frown appeared on Roger's brow.

"How do you know how much time I spend alone in my rooms?" he asked in a surprised voice.

"Oh, these things get around," she answered vaguely.

"Do they? I wonder. I'd like to hazard a guess as to who *your* informant was, at any rate," he said drily.

"You'd probably be right, but let's change the subject. Or rather, let's get back to books."

Even the unvoiced name of Hugh seemed to strike a discordant note. But Roger appeared reluctant to re-open the subject of books. He said nothing at all for a minute or two. When he did speak, it was to ask her if she'd like her coffee in the foyer lounge beside the fire. She said she would, and so they left the table and made their way there.

The waiter brought the coffee, leaving Netta to pour it, and they sat in silence for a while, lost in their own thoughts, Netta thinking of the things they had talked about, and wishing with a longing that hurt, that this could go on for always. What about Iris? she wondered unhappily. Was there any truth in the stories that she and Roger were making plans for marriage?

It was Roger who spoke first, taking up the threads of their earlier conversation, and startling her further.

"Quite seriously," he began, "I'd like to get away from hospital life, Netta."

She stared at him, unable to believe that he was serious, in spite of the way he had prefaced his statement.

"Roger, you—you can't mean it!"

He smiled slightly. "The idea shocks you quite a good deal, doesn't it?"

"But—but way, Roger? Why should you even contemplate such a thing? Do you mean you'd like to go into private practice or something like that?"

"No. I mean giving up practising surgery. It's not that I don't like it or that I'm losing interest either in the job as a skill or helping to ease pain. It's just that—there's something else I want to do, and—well, I am rather tired of the kind of life we lead in hospital socially. Apart from anything else, I'd like a place of my own and the right person to share it with. In other words—marriage."

## CHAPTER EIGHT

"YES, well, of course, that's what we all want, deep lown inside," she heard herself saying in a voice as casual as if his statement was not breaking her heart and as if he meant nothing at all to her, even adding for good measure: "Would you like another cup of coffee?"

She was like a person acting a part. A Punchinello. A person who has caught a glimpse of something unspeakable in a room and slammed the door shut, pretending it wasn't there.

Roger shook his head to more coffee, and in a little while suggested leaving.

"Would you like to do something else to round off the evening? Dancing, for instance?"

She hesitated. Could she really bear to be held closely in his arms that way, knowing he was not in love with her? Then suddenly she smiled. She would take the pain along with the pleasure. She would forget that she meant nothing to him, she would play a game of make-believe.

"Yes, that would be lovely," she said brightly.

He caught her mood. They found a dancing academy where an advanced class was in progress and danced every dance for the next two hours. The first time Roger put his arm about her she had to prevent herself from leaning her head against his chest. But by the time the evening was over, they were both behaving like a couple in love, dancing cheek to cheek, saying nothing, especially during the waltzes.

Netta was transported. She was too bemused to react in any other way, too out-of-this-world to question or analyze. At the back of her mind she knew he was just flirting. But temporary, at least, she didn't mind, didn't care.

At the end of the evening they put on their coats, and he put his arm around her waist as he led her to where he hal parked his car. She sat beside him in a daze, not speaking, as he drove back the way they had come. He did not speak, either, but she was in too much of a dream to notice. Or had she dropped off into a genuine sleep? Whichever way it was, she suddenly realized that Roger was turning the corner of the street where she lived, and the next moment he was pulling up in front of the house.

"Oh dear, I think I must have fallen asleep," she said, apologetically. "Would you like to come up for a drink or anything, Roger?"

He switched off his headlights and stopped the engine. "No, thanks, Netta. I'd rather say goodnight to you down here." He turned in his seat and looked at her. In the dim street lighting, she could just see his face, and her heart contracted violently. *Darling, I love you,* she said silently.

He gave one of his gentle smiles. "It's been a wonderful evening, Netta. I don't know how to thank you."

She shook her head, wanting to weep for a happiness that was not quite happiness.

"There's no need," she told him softly. "I've enjoyed it too much for any thanks to be owed to me."

He leaned towards her, and in a panic now, she hoped he wasn't going to kiss her. But he did, and for a moment there was nothing. No earth, sky, time or consciousness except his lips on hers and a feeling of being suspendel in space. Then it was like a spell being broken. In a split second she saw the whole evening, Iris, Hugh, all Hugh had said and Iris too, and finally that night at the dance when she had been fool enough to fall in love with him because he had kissed her flashed into her mind.

With sudden violence she pushed him away, fumbled with the door handle which mercifully opened easily, and almost fell out of the car. She slammed the door after her, and without looking back ran up the path to the house. Hurriedly, she felt in her bag for her key, ringing the bell of the flat at the same time. But she had no need to fear that Roger was hastening after her. As her hand closed on her key she heard his engine roar into life.

She thrust the key in the lock, all life and feeling draining from her. It wasn't until Elva appeared on the stairs in her dressing gown that she realized what a fool she had been.

"What on earth's the matter?" came Elva's down-to-earth voice. "I thought you'd forgotten your key or something. You must have been in a hurry to get in."

"I was. Sorry to have brought you down."

"That's all right. I wasn't in bed. Just pottering. Did you have a nice evening? Or is that a tactless question?"

Netta followed her into the flat. In a sense, she was thankful for Elva, the way she just said what came into her head. It whittled things down to a normal, ordinary, sensible level.

"It was a wonderful evening," she answered. "We had dinner, then we went dancing. Roger's a wonderful conversationalist."

"What sort of things did you talk about?"

"Oh, this and that, you know. Books, shoes and ships——"

Elva laughed. "Very enlightening. And when he tried to kiss you, you got into a panic and bolted."

Netta sighed. "That's about the size of it." Then she added, with a touch of wry humor: "How'd you guess?"

"How indeed!" answered Elva. "I've got the kettle on. I'll go and make some tea."

Elva proved more understanding than she sometimes seemed. She made the tea and poured it, chattering about her own day, asking Netta no more questions. But then after a while, she said:

"You know, Netta, I don't think there's anything serious between Roger and Iris, otherwise he wouldn't have invited you out tonight—even if Iris did happen to be on duty when he was off."

Netta began to prepare for bed. "That sounds logical enough. But you're judging his behavior by what you believe are normal, ordinary standards, aren't you? Just because he took me out to dinner, that's not to say he isn't planning to marry Iris. In fact," she added, remembering what he had said, "I think it's very likely true."

"But that would make him the unfaithful type!" protested Elva.

"Not necessarily. Who knows what motives men have for what they do? They're very fond of

141

accusing women of being illogical and so on. But men take a bit of understanding, too, at times."

"How right you are!" answered Elva with feeling.

The two then lapsed into silence. Netta didn't know quite what to make of Roger and some of the things he had said. Had she been intended to take seriously his views about a surgeon's job, his hint that he might be leaving the hospital and taking up other work? But what other kind of work could he possibly mean? Surely he had been just talking for talking's sake, making conversation?

She turned wearily on the pillow. She was rapidly becoming exhausted emotionally. The whole situation was getting beyond her. She couldn't stand it much longer. She would have to leave. She had been a fool to go out with Roger this evening, of course. She might have known it would bring her little else but heartache. But she had been unable to resists the temptation, and it really had been wonderful—to a point. She had tried not to fight against love, but there were other things one had to fight, too, and they were not so easy. One of these was the desire and the longing to be loved in return. Everyone in love reached this phase sooner or later. The desire to tell of one's love to the person concerned became urgent, too, after a while, coupled with that most fundamental of all needs—the need to give expression to the love. These were the things which caused the frustrations and the sufferings of those in love.

Netta knew that her work would begin to suffer before long if she could not cope with her feelings. Before that could be allowed to happen, she must take steps to find another post. Her thoughts went vaguely to the jobs overseas she had been contemplating applying for. Tomorrow, she decided, she would take another look at some of them. And with this thought she drifted into sleep.

When she went on duty the next morning, the unit was as busy as she had ever seen it. The theatre was being prepared for an amputation. A middle-aged industrial worked had caught his leg in some machinery, and immediate surgery had been advised by the consultant orthopaedic surgeon. The patient's wife and other relatives were there, and the surgeon was trying to explain to them why such a drastic step as amputation was necessary.

"It would be hopeless to try to do anything else," he said as gently as he could. "There's far too much damage, both to bone and tissue. Believe me, I'd save his leg, if I could." He showed them the X-ray picture. "You see? The upper part of the leg below the knee—the tibia and fibula are absolutely in fragments. Anything we tried to do in the way of reduction and grafting and so on would take years. And even after all the suffering he would have to undergo, he'd still be left with a pretty useless, and what's more, painful limb. You understand? He wouldn't be able to do even the lightest job, still less enjoy living. And in the end, he'd have to have his leg amputated. Whereas, if we do it now—much as we dislike having to do it —in about eighteen months' time he'll be walking as well as you or I."

There was a silence while his wife wiped her eyes and along with his other relatives, thought about the matter.

"Well, if it's got to be done, it has, that's all," his wife said, a sob in her voice. "It's—a terrible thing, but I wouldn't like to see him suffer to try to save it, if what you say is true—and I'm sure it is."

"You can take my word for it, Mrs. Wood," the surgeon said gently, and went on to explain more fully the step-by-step progress of what her husband's treatment would be.

"But what about Harold—my husband? Does he understand?"

"Yes, I think so, although, of course, he's still in a lot of pain. He didn't like the idea of losing his leg, naturally, and he wanted to know how you felt about it before he agreed. I think you can help him. You're a very brave woman, Mrs. Wood. Go and talk to him, encourage him. As a matter of fact, I saw a man in Out-patients only yesterday who had had an amputation. He walked in without even the aid of his sticks. You'd hardly have known that his legs weren't both his own."

Mrs. Wood gave a watery smile. "And if he has it done, how soon will he be home, doctor?"

"If all goes well, he should be home before Christmas. He'll be on crutches, of course, and his wound may not be quite healed, but the district nurse will take care of that. Then he'll attend Out-patients until he gets his artificial limb and he's thoroughly used to it."

Five minutes later the anaesthetic consent form was signed, and Mr. Wood was given his pre-operative drug.

Hugh scrubbed up to give the intravenous anaesthetic. Netta said good morning to him, but his answer was very brusque. But Netta had no time to wonder why, apart from the fact that she had told him she didn't want to see him again. Both she and Staff Nurse Kelly scrubbed up for the operation, and the consultant was assited by Stephen Monro, and Bob Griffiths, who wanted to specialize in orthopaedic surgery.

The next case was one for Roger. He came into the theatre suddenly, and at the sight of him, Netta's heart contracted painfully.

"Laparotomy, Sister," he said in a quiet voice. "Pancreas involved almost certainly. Probably liver and intestines, too."

She glanced at him, but his expression was withdrawn, and almost before he had finished speaking he had turned away. Netta's whole being was heavy with tears she could not shed. She must get away, she must. Of course he was angry with her, and she could hardly blame him. Throughout the day he seemed dominated by a kind of cold but carefully controlled anger.

"A drunken driver knocked this man down on a pedestrian crossing," he said to Jerry during the laparotomy. "The word 'accident' should be scrubbed out of the dictionary. In nine case out of ten they're no such thing—or ninety-nine out of a hundred. If I had my way, those sort of drivers would have their licences taken away for good."

"Drastic," muttered Jerry.

"Not half drastic enough."

Netta noticed Hugh watching him covertly, a gleam of wicked humor and speculation in his eyes.

"Well, well,' he said eventually, as Roger went out in answer to his lights. "Didn't he get much of his own way last night, then, Netta?"

Netta colored angrily. "That kind of question is best ignored!"

Jerry's dark brows shot up. "What's this? I didn't know you and the Chief were going out together, Netta."

"We're not," she told him. "He asked me out to dinner last night, that's all. And we had a very pleasant evening," she added defiantly, looking at Hugh.

"Really?" he said mockingly. "Well, something's upset him, obviously."

"Are you always bright and smiling and good-tempered?" she flung back at him. "Not", she amended, "that he's been bad-tempered exactly."

"But you can't say he's been sunny either, can you? Not that it worries me any," said Hugh, with a barely concealed smile.

Netta looked at him steadily, coming near to loathing him. "You hate Roger, don't you, Hugh? Just exactly how many lies have you told about him? How many people's minds have you poisoned against him?"

Hugh's eyes narrowed. "Ah, he makes me sick. I'll tell you something, shall I? A friend of mine was engaged—and Henderson broke it up between them, then left the girl flat. That's the kind of man he is, and I'm telling you the truth. Believe me, if that man doesn't leave here soon, I shall. Because I can't stand the sight of him!"

He flung down his mask and thrust his way through the swing doors of the anaesthetic room. Netta picked up the discarded regalia in silence. Jerry gave her a questioning glance.

"What's it all about, Netta?" he asked quietly.

She heaved a great sigh. "I just don't want to talk about it, Jerry, if you don't mind."

"Why? Because you're personally involved? You are, aren't you, Netta?"

"The nurses are waiting to mop up, Jerry," she answered, and make her escape.

That evening when she went off duty, Netta wrote a letter in answer to one of the advertisements for overseas State Registered Nurses. A few days later, she had a reply enclosing a form of questionnaire to fill in, and within the week, she was asked to go to London for an interview. It was then that she went to see Matron to inform her of her plans. Matron was shocked and dismayed.

"But why, Sister? I thought you were happy and settled at the Centre."

"Yes, I was, Matron, but for purely personal reasons, I feel I must get away now."

Matron eyed her steadily. "I shall have difficulty in replacing you, Sister. Are you sure you won't change your mind? Is there nothing I can either say or do which will help?"

"No, Matron. I'm sorry."

Matron shook her head regretfully. "Well, let me know how you get on, and if you do change your mind——"

Netta thanked her once more and went out. She wasn't happy about leaving, by any means, but there was a point at which one had to admit failure or be guilty of stubborn self-will and foolishness.

"Going by car, are you?" queried Elva the previous evening, as Netta pinned up her hair.

"Why not? The interview isn't until the afternoon. If I start out early I shall just about make it."

"It's a long way, though. You haven't done much long-distance driving, have you?"

"What's the difference? If I feel tired, I can pull in somewhere and rest a while. And I'm not going to take the car into London. I shall drive to Watford like Jerry and I did a couple of times, then leave the car in the station car park and take the Underground the rest of the way."

"Does Roger know you're planning to leave?" Elva asked, after a while.

"No. Nobody knows except you and Matron."

"Not even Jerry?"

"Not even Jerry!"

Netta rose early the next morning, and made sandwiches and a flask of coffee so that she wouldn't have to take up time having lunch at a restaurant. She had filled the tank full of petrol the night before, and knew, approximately, how far it would take her. She had determined never to let herself run out of petrol again since that night Roger had had to tow her in.

She drove carefully, and when she joined the M.I, kept in the slow lane until she felt confident, looking well in her mirror before pulling out to overtake the slow-moving traffic. It had been a fair enough morning when she set out, cold, but fine, and after a while the sun came out. But then a haze covered the sun as if a giant had breathed over it, on a frosty morning, and soon Netta found herself driving through mist patches. She dropped her speed. She had seen too many tragic results from this motorway to take any risks. As on an ordinary road, she tried to keep a safe distance between herself and the vehicle ahead, but it was difficult. In spite of the mist patches, cars zoomed passed at sixty or seventy miles an hour, and no sooner had she slowed down to keep a reasonable distance from the car in front than another one slipped in between. Would motorists never learn? she wondered. The motorways were wonderful, especially on a long journey. There were no traffic lights or roundabouts to hold you up, you didn't have to crawl for miles of bends behind heavy, slow-moving traffic if you didn't want to. You could keep up a steady speed which took hours off a journey. But because of this, and because many modern cars were built for speeds far in excess of what the human brain could adequately cope with, all these terrible accidents occurred, leaving people injured and perhaps in pain for the rest of their lives, leaving children without fathers, wives without husbands.

Now, once more, the mist had reached out its ghostly fingers, pulling herself and the car in front swiftly into its obscurity. Cautiously, Netta eased her foot off the accelerator pedal.

Then, with a sudden, shattering violence, there came from somewhere ahead in the treacherous centre of the mist the ominous sound of breaking glass and metal on metal. Netta's right foot transferred instinctively to the brake pedal. At the same moment the brake lights of the car in front showed red.

The next second or two was a blur. Time telescoped. Into Netta's mind flashed all the accident cases she had ever seen, all the advice she had ever heard. Then somehow she was oddly calm, her brain startlingly clear. She was *in* the drama of a motorway pile-up, not merely seeing the tragic results.

The car in front of her suddenly swerved to the right to avoid collision. At the precise moment, Netta wrenched at the wheel and swerved to the left, pushing her foot hard on the brake. Then the air was filled with the most horrible, ghastly sounds. A sickening crash as two cars collided violently, brakes screeching, people shouting. Hell let loose.

Netta felt her own car spin round frighteningly before, somehow, she brought it to a screaming halt. For a moment she leaned over the wheel, trembling, her eyes closed. Then realization came to her. She was still alive. Alive and uninjured. How had the miracle happened? And why?

Fearfully, she glanced around, and as her eyes met the devastation, she felt sick. A car coming up on the fast lane, obviously at speed, had collided with the one which had swerved to the right, with the result that several cars were heaped together in a ghastly, appalling conglomeration of metal and humanity. What she had seen in theatre was nothing compared with this.

She reached for the first-aid kit she had recently started carrying around in her car and had climbed slowly out. The dead she could do nothing for. The shocked and injured she could perhaps help. She stood for a moment, wondering where to begin. From left to right as far as could be seen in the mist, one car was locked with another in a seemingly never-ending, higgledy-piggledy line.

Other people—mainly men—began to stagger from their cars. From another, Netta heard a groan. She hurried towards the sound. Someone else could notify the police, send for ambulances.

Her job was to do what she could here and now.

Four men were in the car to which Netta went. The two in the front were unconscious, their windscreen shattered. The two at the back were conscious, but their legs were trapped between the back of the front seat and their own. The rear of the car was caved in, and the two would be lucky if they had escaped spinal injuries. Her first-aid equipment seemed hopelessly inadequate. There was little she could do for the two men until the cars were separated one from the other all along the line.

Netta began to feel desperate. Then a man with blood running down his face came up to her.

"I don't know who you are, miss, but if that's a first-aid kit you've got there, there's a man in that long red car"—he pointed—"who looks as if he might be bleeding to death."

He looked pretty shocked himself, but Netta went quickly to the car he had indicated. Here she found a man who was bleeding profusely from the neck. From the way the blood was coming in spurts, and from its color, an artery had been pierced by a piece of glass from the smashed-in windscreen. She applied digital pressure above the wound on the carotid artery. But this was the most difficult place of all to apply adequate pressure, and guessing that any small fragments of glass would have been washed out of the wound by this time, she applied a gauze pad, and bandaged it on as firmly as possible.

From one car to another she went, giving first-aid where it was most urgently needed. The police arrived and cleared a way for the rest of the traffic, taking names and addresses of those injured, then directing ambulances as they arrived. Netta helped by pointing out which of the cases she had tended were the most urgent in need of hospital treatment, so that they could be taken without delay. Two of these were small children, and it was heartbreaking to see their limp little forms being carried into the ambulance.

The majority of these injured people would be taken to her own hospital, to the Emergency Centre, if not all. She visualized the scene. It would be hectic. She should be there with them. They would need every pair of hands they could get. But so many cars had been involved in this pile-up. She felt certain it would turn out to have been the worst ever. There were still people requiring first-aid treatment.

She decided to stay until the next ambulance had been and gone then return to the hospital. Perhaps she could take one or two people with her. With regard to her appointment, she would never get there in time now. And even if it had been possible, she wouldn't have had the heart to continue the journey after all this. She would have to ring the Overseas Nursing Association when she arrived back at the hospital.

The next ambulance came, and the worst of the remaining cases were carried into it. Netta went and spoke to the police sergeant in charge. By this time he knew who she was. She told him of her plan, and he thanked her.

"I don't know what some of these people would have done without you, Sister," he said. "You've been absolutely splendid."

"I'm glad I happened to be on the spot. But which of these people do you think I can take with me?"

They were discussing the matter when a second ambulance drove up. The door was opened by the driver, and to Netta's surprise Jerry stepped out, a worried, anxious look on his face.

He stopped short at the sight of Netta, and his expression changed to one of infinite relief. He came towards her slowly, and the look of tenderness in his eyes was something Netta would never forget.

"Netta. Oh, *Netta!* Thank God you're safe!"

Then with a rush he took the next few steps and caught her in his arms and held her to him as though he would never let her go.

## CHAPTER NINE

FOR a moment Netta clung to him. "Jerry! Oh, I'm glad you've come. It's—it's been terrible, simply terrible."

His hold tightened even more for a second, then he relaxed a little, touching her hair, comforting her.

"There, there now," he said huskily. "Don't give way after being so brave. Not that I'd blame you if you did. But come away out of it now. You must be needing some shock treatment yourself after all you've been doling out. One of the ambulance drivers told us you were here, and what you were doing. Where's your car? Is it damaged?"

She shook her head and pointed, then suddenly became aware of the police sergeant standing beside them.

"Sorry about this, Sergeant," she said a little self-consciously.

"You go now, Sister," he urged. "You've done enough, and we've been right glad of it. Don't bother taking anyone with you. We can pile plenty of sitting patients in the next ambulance."

"Quite right," said Jerry. "Come along now. And I'm doing the driving."

His arm about her shoulders, Jerry led her to where her car was standing. It wasn't until she sank into the passenger seat that she realized what a strain the last two or three hours had been. She reached out for Jerry's hand, feeling near to tears.

"Jerry, there's no one in the world I'd rather have seen than you, just now."

He turned in his seat and gave her a long look. "Bless you for that, Netta."

He turned the car around and started off back to Witteringham. "I'm getting off this motorway as soon as possible," he said. "You've had enough of it for a while, I should think."

She was thankful when he did. She would drive along it again, of course. One could not stay afraid for ever. But it would be a long time, if ever, before she would drive along it during misty or foggy weather.

"You should have gone by train, of course," Jerry told her severely. "And if I'd known you'd been contemplating any such journey——"

He left the sentence unfinished. Netta thought how much he had changed these last few months. He had become older somehow, with an older man's wisdom and thoughtfulness. Elva's influence, probably. When he and herself had been going out together he had been—or had seemed to be—so gay and lighthearted as to appear almost irresponsible. But they both had, she reflected ruefully. Was it love that had made them become more mature? There could be few things which brought greater suffering than unrequited love, apart from physical pain, though some who had not experienced it would argue differently.

But really, love was the most vital element in the whole of human existence, a fundamental need of everyone, no matter how hard-bitten or self-sufficient they considered themselves. Even physical pain that no drug could touch was made easier to bear by the love of another. The rejection of one's love, whether by man, woman or child, was one of life's major tragedies.

"All right?" Jerry asked her presently.

She hauled herself out of her thoughts. "Oh, yes, thanks, Jerry."

He flashed her a smile. "You were so quiet, I thought you'd gone to sleep."

"Not quite, but very nearly," she answered.

They were off the motorway now and on one of the arterial roads which wind leisurely for miles, or if you are in a hurry, wind frustratingly.

"You won't have had any lunch, I suppose," said Jerry.

"No, but that reminds me. I've got sandwiches and a flask of coffee in the back."

"You need something a little more substantial than that. And above all, you need to get out of this car for a little while."

"But, Jerry, don't you think we ought to get back to the Centre as quickly as possible? They must be up to their eyes and ears there. In fact, I can't imagine why Roger let you come at all."

Jerry gave an explosive laugh. "Neither Roger nor anyone else could have stopped me, even if they'd wanted to—which they didn't. Then, more soberly, "You have simply no idea, Netta, how worried we all were when Elva told us where you'd gone."

"But I might not have been anywhere near the pile-up!"

"Do you think that made anyone feel any better? Anyway, to get back to the point in question: I am not taking you back there without something to eat inside you, so you can stop arguing. Besides which, I need to telephone. I promised I would to let them know whether you were all right."

It gave Netta a wonderful warm feeling that they had all been so concerned about her.

"Do you know what I'd like more than anything else, Jerry?" she said suddenly.

"Name it, and it's yours," he told her.

"A cup of tea."

"Well, that shouldn't be too difficult," he said with a grin.

About another three miles farther along, they came across a likely-looking hotel, and pulled into the parking area. There was a pleasant lounge-foyer and a bright fire burning, so Jerry directed Netta to sit there while he spoke to the proprietor. In a very short time a pot of tea was brought to her.

"Now you just sit there and drink it, and I'll go and phone the hospital," Jerry ordered.

Netta was deeply touched by his kindness. She reflected that both of them were ready for marriage in a way they had never been before. But she thrust such thoughts aside. Elva was in love with Jerry, and he possibly, with her. Today he was just being kind, and, of course, still had a certain fondness for her. But that was all.

After a minute or two he returned, saying how pleased everyone was back at the Centre, and that he was to see that she had some lunch.

"Roger doesn't think you should go on duty, if that's what you had in mind," he added.

"Why doesn't he?" she asked in a flat voice.

"He thinks you've had enough for one day, I suppose."

Netta asked Jerry if he would like some tea, but he declined, and as she had had enough, they went into the hotel's restaurant for lunch.

When they were nearing the outskirts of town, Jerry tried to dissuade her from going on duty.

"After all, we've had these pile-ups before, you know," he told her.

"But not as bad as this," she protested. "And I've usually been on duty, anyway. In fact I can't remember there being anything like this ever.

"Look, Netta, if you hadn't been involved, you might have been in London and totally unaware of what had happened, and by the time you got back it would have all been over."

"Is there some other reason why you don't want me to come? I expect you can manage perfectly well without me," she finished, wistfully.

"Now you're being an idiot. It was chaotic when I left, and I expect it still is. I know several people who'd give three hearty cheers if you were to walk in, but——"

"Then it's settled," she said happily. "Let me just call at the flat for my uniform and I'll be with you in two minutes flat."

"Why can't I keep my big mouth shut?" he groaned.

Organized chaos was more accurate, naturally, for the state of things at the Emergency Centre. Reception, Recovery and Resuscitation were working at full pressure. Netta had certainly never seen anything like it. Elva, too, was busy in the plaster room. The door was open, and Netta looked in for a moment. Rubber gloves on, Elva was smoothing plaster of Paris over an injured wrist.

"Netta! Heavens, am I glad to see you. We've been having kittens here, I can tell you. Honestly, my heart turned over when cases began to come in and I realized you might have run into it. According to Jerry, you've had an absolutely miraculous escape."

"Yes. See you later, Elva. I'll go and see if I can give a hand in theatre."

Netta went into the nurses' changing room and put on a gown and mask, then went into the theatre. Roger was at the operating table and was putting the final sutures into an abdominal wound.

He had just finished tying the last but one, and was holding it up for Joe Griffiths to cut. As Netta came in he looked up and his eyes met hers in a direct look.

"Hello, Sister. Glad to see you back all safe and sound. You shouldn't really have come on duty, but we could certainly do with some help."

Hugh, at the patient's head, stood up from his stool. "It seems you have a charmed life, Netta. Jerry says you had a lucky escape. How'd you manage it?"

But Netta replied only briefly. At the instrument trolley, Nurse Lewis looked almost fit to drop, and on making an enquiry, Netta discovered that the girl had not eaten since breakfast.

"Then go now, right away, Nurse," she told her. "And on your way back ask at the kitchen if we can have a supply of sandwiches." She turned to Roger, who was now stripping off his gloves. "I don't suppose you've had lunch, either, have you, Mr. Henderson?"

"You suppose right, Sister. I'll be glad of one of those sandwiches when Staff Nurse gets back. Meanwhile, I'm wanted in Resuscitation."

At this, Netta decided to telephone the kitchen instead of having Nurse Lewis call, and went to the surgeons' changing room to make sure there was an adequate supply of coffee brewing, feeling almost guilty that she and Jerry had lingered to have a proper lunch.

Netta scrubbed up for the next case, the orthopaedic specialist operating, Stephen Monro assisting. It was one of the children Netta had watched being carried into the ambulance. The child was still deeply unconscious, having numerous lacerations of the face, fractured ribs, and possibly a fractured skull.

"It's criminal! If only some of the people who take such appalling risks on the roads could see the results of their actions," lamented the surgeon.

"I rather think, sir, that one of them in this instance is dead," remarked Netta in a flat voice.

"I'm not surprised. The trouble is, today's cars are built for speed, but man isn't."

"I couldn't agree more," said Stephen Monro. "But I'd go even further. In my opinion the greater proportion of so-called accidents are caused by faults in character. It's the man at the wheel rather than his machine. Netta's escape might be a miracle in one way, but I'd like to guarantee that it was as much to do with her care, her patience, her sense of responsibility and conscientious driving as anything else. Some of these maniacs on the road are murderers—and worse. The maddening things is, we've got a waiting list of patients requiring arthroplasty, and while they're waiting, they're in contiual pain. Meanwhile, the beds are being taken up day after day with these road accidents that could be avoided.

As was the way of some surgeons, the orthopaedic specialist continued to talk as he operated, alternating what had to be said about the patient's treatment with talk of the day's accidents.

"Tell us about it, Sister, if you can bear to. What action did you take? And what happened, exactly?"

As briefly as she could, Netta told them how she had tried to keep a safe distance between her car and the one in front and how she had slowed down in good time, then about the car which came up on the fast lane, colliding with the other one."

"It was this mist, you see. One minute it was clear, then——"

"But surely nobody should be taken unawares as much as all that, with all the propaganda on television," Hugh protested. "The point is, if more people had slowed down as Netta did, there probably would have been no pile-up at all. And if that idiot hadn't tried to overtake at speed there would certainly have been no deaths. Ugh! It makes you sick to think of it."

Netta stayed on duty quite late that evening. As well as the casualties from the motor accident there were other emergencies, too, including two acute abdomens and a child with severe burns caused by wearing one of the old type of flammable nightdresses. One of these was the last operation before the night staff came on. Roger stripped off his gloves and gown with a gesture of utter weariness.

"A cup of coffee, Mr. Henderson?" asked Netta.

He took a deep breath and let it out again slowly. Then he managed a faint smile.

"I've drunk enough coffee today to sink a ship. I think I'd like something stronger." He paused, then added: "How about coming to have one with me?"

Her eyes widened in swift surprise. After the way she had behaved the evening when he had taken her out to dinner, she thought he would be too angry with her ever to suggest anything else. Even as an inner voice warned her against it, she found herself accepting.

"I think I'd like that, Mr. Henderson."

He looked at her thoughtfully. "Why the formality? I thought we were friends?"

She colored. "I—thought perhaps after last time, you——"

His lips quirked. "Don't let that worry you. I don't blame you. Maybe I should have asked your permission before taking such a liberty. But then it wouldn't have been a liberty, would it?"

"No, I—I suppose not."

He could poke about it, of course. It meant nothing to him. Some of the things Hugh said about him were true. He was a flirt. And yet——

"Well then, I'll see you in about—what? Five minutes? You're not staying to do any clearing up or anything, are you?" She shook her head. "Right. In five minutes, then, at the side entrance."

He went off, and she turned as a hand touched her arm. It was Jerry.

"Making an assignation or something?" he asked.

She gave him an apologetic look, not quite sure where she and Jerry stood with each other after this afternoon's incident.

"He asked me to have a drink with him. It seemed—churlish to refuse."

He shrugged. "All right. I just wondered if you'd like me to run you home. I'm going to the flat, anyway. Elva wants a lift. I might see you, if he's not too late bringing you home." He smiled and hugged her shoulders. "Have a nice time. Just relax and don't worry too much. Roger's all right. One of the best."

What did he mean by 'relax and don't worry too much? she wondered, as she did what she had to do before handing over to the night staff nurse. And what made him remark that Roger was all right? Suddenly she felt awfully tired. Perhaps there had been nothing in it at all.

She left her collar and cuffs hanging up in the changing room, and put on her outdoor uniform coat, then slipped out of the side entrance. Roger was waiting lor her, and put a hand under her arm.

"Ah, there you are. This way."

He steered her in the direction of the residents' block.

"But I've got my car round the other side——"
she began.

"We're not going anywhere by car," he told her.
"Certainly not to the Cheshire Cheese."

"Then where?"

"To my rooms. I just want to relax in a comfortable chair, and I'm quite sure you do, too. I'll drive you to the flat a little later on when I'm fortified."

"But—are you sure it will be all right? I mean——"

"I simply don't care whether it's all right or not—unless you should strongly object. Don't worry. I'll ring the Super and let him know I've got a visitor."

Netta made no further protest. In general, the residents' block was out of bounds to the nursing staff, but exceptions were made from time to time with regard to the senior staff, so she supposed it would be all right. She was really filled with curiosity as to what his rooms would be like. The furniture would not be his, of course, but his personality would be there.

As it happened, they met nobody on the way, and reached the door of his rooms without seeing anyone, too.

"It's like that sometimes," he said, as he turned the knob of his door and found it unlocked. "Another time, you run into everybody."

"Don't you lock your door?" she asked him.

"When I think about it," he answered casually. "People in general are trustworthy enough, and I don't have any valuables. Money I carry around with me, but I don't keep much cash on hand. The bank isn't far and the general office never mind cashing a cheque."

He stepped inside the room and switched on the light. "Come along in. It's not what you might call palatial, but at least there are a couple of comfortable chairs, and we can relax."

161

Netta looked around. The furnishings and so on were not his choice, but it was a typically masculine room. There were few pictures or ornaments, chairs were thrust back and left where they had been pushed, books and newspapers were on almost every chair, and a desk in one corner was absolutely littered with papers.

"I wouldn't get a prize for tidiness, would I?" he grinned. "How'd you like to take me in hand, Netta?" As he spoke, he took off his raincoat and flung it on to a chair.

Netta tightened her defences around her. "I'm afraid I wouldn't be much use," she told him. "I'm not a very tidy person myself."

"I'm sure that's not true," he said. He switched on an electric fire with a log effect. "There, that'll look a bit more cheerful. There is some central heating, as you've probably noticed, but I don't like a room with no fire at all, even if it's only an artificial one."

"Neither do I."

"So that's one thing we have in common, isn't it? But look, let me take your coat, then sit down and make yourself comfortable and tell me what you'd like to drink."

She relinquished her coat and sat down. "That depends on what you've got to offer," she answered, trying to respond to his mood.

"You name it, I've got it—almost."

She settled for a sherry, and he poured himself out a small whisky and sat lown in a chair opposite her. He sipped at his drink, then gave a contented sigh, stretching out his leg.

"Ah, this is better, and I must say it's nice to see you sitting there."

"Thank you," she said in a surprised voice.

"I would have asked you before, but I didn't think you'd come," he went on.

"Then——"

"Why have I now?" He grinned. "Let's say I'm getting hard-faced."

His manner was so casual, so carefree in comparison with what she was feeling, she felt she would scream. She sipped her sherry and looked into the fire. Why had she come? she thought numbly. As soon as she could, she would make her excuses. She looked up, and her eye caught the desk again.

"You look as though you've been busy," she said, hoping to embark on a less dangerous topic. "Are you studying for something?"

He turned his head and looked towards the desk. "Hardly. Guess again."

"Well, the only other thing I can think of is that you must be writing a book."

He inclined his head and eyed her. "That's right. Like to glance at some of it? Tell me what you think."

Netta frowned. "You're joking. You must be."

"Why so?"

She stared at him. "You mean, you really are writing a book?"

"Yes." Then he smiled a little. "That's why I'm so 'unsociable'. I'll get you the first chapter. I'd like to know what you think of it."

He went over to the desk, and out of the seeming chaos picked a neatly clipped, typed sheaf of manuscript. Netta could barely take this in. He had kept it such a close secret, she had never dreamed of such a thing.

"Here you are," he said, handing her the portion of manuscript. "I'm having it typed as I complete each chapter so that I can judge how it's going. I might say you're the first to see it."

"Really?" She took it from him wonderingly. "I'm honored. But why should I be so privileged?"

"I'll tell you some time. But not now. Anyway, it might not be such a privilege. Wait until you've read a bit of it. One reason why I've picked on you is that I know you'll be honest, of course. Now, just pretend you've got this book out of the library. Or better still, pretend you're in the library and you've just taken this down from the shelf. Read a page or so and tell me whether you'd want to take it home or just put it back on the shelf."

She smiled at him. "All right. But promise there'll be no hard feelings if I do put it back on the shelf?"

"None whatever, especially if you can tell me why."

He went back to his chair and picked up a newspaper. Netta bent her head to the typescript and began to read. It had no title as yet, but Netta found the very first line arresting.

*A man stood on the deck of a ship just coming in to harbor. This was not just the end of a long and strange journey, but the beginning of a new and perhaps equally strange life. What would he find in this foreign country, who meet?*

She read on, absorbed, as the gist of the theme began to filter through, and before she realized it, she had come to the end of the chapter. She looked up to see Roger's eyes fixed upon her, an expression on his face she had never seen before.

"So you read to the end of the chapter," he said quietly. "I find that gratifying. What do you think of it?"

Their eyes met for a moment, and in the look something was born between them. It had nothing to do with the love Netta had for him. It was greater than that. A spark of something. An understanding. She couldn't describe it. She couldn't comprehend it—yet.

164

"I think it's great, Roger. The theme, the writing—everything. If you can write like this why——"

He interrupted. "Why am I practising surgery? That's what I was getting at the other evening. Remember? But I didn't really know what I was writing was any good. I felt it was myself. But it's difficult to be objective about one's own work."

She did remember. His opinion that one craft was as good as another. That if a person like a surgeon felt he could do something else equally well——

"What I was going to say, Roger, was—if you can write like this, why haven't you done so before?"

He smiled. "But, Netta, this hasn't happened suddenly, overnight. I've been writing on and off for—well years, I suppose."

"You mean you've written other books?"

He shook his head. "Not other books. For years I kept a diary, still do, as a matter of fact. Not just a three-line-a-day affair, of course."

"More a sort of journal?"

"That's right. In it, I recorded impressions of people I met, thought things out, described places where I'd been and so on. Then I began making up stories around people I knew. The thing is, there's a story in everyone's life, and I'm very interested in people, interested in what makes them act the way they do."

"More interested than in saving life?"

He frowned. "Does it have to be such a clear-cut alternative? Of course I'm interested in saving life, but as I tried to explain the other evening, aren't we sometimes hog-tied, hide-bound or whatever, by ideals that are traditional—habit—rather than what we feel? But some of these traditions are so long-standing and inbred, it's often difficult to decide what *is* the right thing to do.

165

Netta began to speak, then checked her tongue just in time. *Darling,* she almost said. "I think I know your difficulty."

"You were about to say?" he prompted.

If only he knew! "Only that I—think I know what your difficulty is. You're torn between surgery and your writing, between your present career and what might be a new one, what you'd *like* to be your new one, aren't you?"

"That's about the size of it."

"Is the novel finished?"

"Nearly. But I've already got another one simmering. To be honest, the writing has the greater pull nowadays. When I'm not doing it, I'm itching to get at it. I forget it when I'm faced with a patient, naturally, and when I'm actually operating. But otherwise, the desire to get back to it is always there."

Netta frowned. "Roger, forgive me, but I can't help thinking that it would be wrong of you to give up surgery entirely. Yet you can't be continually torn like this. The point is, surgeon's are not two a penny. You've spent years acquiring your skill, and such a skill is vitally needed. Witness only today's pile-up. At the same time, the world needs writers, too, especially the kind of writer you are evidently going to be, if I'm any judge."

He grinned. "I think your judgement is excellent! But go on. I'm sure there's more to come, and I'm all ears."

"I'm really trying to sort things out. And what I'm going to say next is so obvious, I don't know what all the talk has been about. You don't have to give up one job for another. You want more time for writing, don't you? I think you ought to have it. The only solution is to set up in a private practice and be available as a consultant in general surgery. You have all the qualifications, and——"

She broke off at the changing expressions on his face.

"Netta that's brilliant," he said. "So obvious, as you say. I've been indulging in wishful thinking rather than the concrete kind. All the same, I can see one or two snags in your idea."

"Such as?"

"Well—for one thing, suppose nobody wants to consult me?"

"But of course they will."

"I may not get many private patients, either."

"Of course it will take a little time, but——"

"In the meantime, I shall suffer a considerable financial loss."

She felt a swift twinge of disappointment in him. "Roger, I don't understand you. Wouldn't it be worthwhile a little sacrifice?"

"It depends on who and what would be sacrificed. You see, I—want to get married, too. I could hardly ask someone else to make sacrifices on my behalf."

Something inside her curled up, but she pretended to ignore it. "I see. I—didn't realize. But surely she'd understand?"

He was eyeing her steadily now, his face grave. "Maybe she would. But have I the right to ask her?"

She stared at him. "You mean—you haven't asked her yet—to marry you?"

"Not yet, no."

"But she—she knows you're—she knows how you feel about her?"

"I haven't told her, if that's what you mean. If I told her that, it would be the equivalent of a proposal of marriage, wouldn't it? So you see my difficulty?" He smiled and leaned forward in his chair. "You've given me some very good advice this evening, Netta. Give me a little more. Do you think I should tell her?"

But this was too much for Netta. She held out the chapter of his novel to him, and rose to her feet.

"I think you've had quite enough of my advice for one evening, Roger. I must go now. I really am tired. But thanks for telling me about the book and everything, and thanks, too, for the drink."

He rose, too, and touched her lightly on the shoulder. "You look tired, I must say. I shouldn't have kept you so long. Selfish of me. I was so full of my own affairs I forgot, for the moment, all you'd been through today. I'll drive you home."

"No, no, really. I can drive myself to the flat. It's not far."

He helped her on with her coat, and in spite of her protests, walked with her to where her car was parked. He didn't speak until they were approaching the car, then he said:

"Let me have your key, Netta, and I'll unlock the door for you."

Thinking he wanted to do the polite thing and hold it open for her, she gave him the key, but to her surprise, when he had unlocked the door he stepped swiftly into the driving seat.

"Get in the other side," he said. "And don't argue. I'm driving. I want to make sure you arrive safely."

There seemed little point in arguing as he was so determined. Now Netta felt so weary she could cry. Roger drove in complete silence, and she was glad. She felt words would have choked her.

"Now show me where the garage is," he said when they arrived at the house, "and I'll run it in for you."

She showed him, and tried to thank him, but he answered gruffly:

"That's all right. It's the very least I can do. Don't hang around. Off you go up to the flat. I'll do the rest."

Feeling considerably deflated as well as tired, she said goodnight and let herself into the house. This was one of the occasions when she wished she didn't share the flat. She just didn't want to talk to anyone. All she wanted to do was crawl into bed and probably cry herself to sleep. But Jerry was in the flat as well as Elva.

"Well, hello there," grinned Jerry. "I knew you'd come home some time or other."

"Hello, Jerry," she answered dispiritedly.

"She's worn out," Elva said. "Push off now, Jerry. Netta's off tomorrow, too. You can come and talk to her then. That is, if she'll have you."

Netta gave a tired smile. "Come any time you like, Jerry. I shan't be going anywhere."

He said it would be some time during the afternoon, and Elva saw him out.

"Thanks, Elva," Netta said when she returned. "I didn't want to talk any more tonight, not even to Jerry."

"I know. And I'm not going to keep you up talking, either. Just get into bed and I'll bring you a hot drink and a biscuit. I don't somehow think you're going to need any sleeping tablets."

Elva was right. She didn't. After the delicious milky hot chocolate Elva brought her, she fell into an exhausted sleep. It was not until she was disturbed by Elva moving about the flat the next morning that she began to dream as she drifted off into a doze again. She dreamed she was nothing more than one of the characters in Roger's book, that he was peering down on to the page of type where she lay unable to move. Iris was there, looking over his shoulder. Then she shook her head, put forward her hand and suddenly closed the book with a slam. Netta felt herself suffocating, and tried to open the book again, but it was too heavy. Then suddenly she realized she was only

169

dreaming and tried to wake herself up. She struggled and struggled, trying to shout, but no sound would come. Then she felt a hand on her shoulder and opened her eyes to see Mrs. Morney bending over her.

"Wake up, my dear, wake up. It's all right now, it's all right."

"Oh, thanks, Mrs. Morney. I was having the most awful dream."

"And no wonder either, after all you went through yesterday! Look, I've brought you some tea and the papers. Now that it's past and done with, you can read all about it. It was a terrible thing, Miss Rowland, and a mercy you weren't killed or at least injured."

Netta sat up. "Oh, Mrs. Morney, this *is* good of you," she said, catching sight of the tea tray. "Thanks very much indeed. I don't really think I want to read about the accident, but it'll be nice to be able to lie and read the rest of the news while I drink my tea."

"There's quite a bit in about you," Mrs. Morney told her. "But I'll leave you to look at in in peace."

Netta thanked her again and poured out a cup of tea, then opened one of the papers.

"Good heavens!" she exclaimed aloud. Her own photograph leaped out of the pages at her, and banner headlines read:

NURSING SISTER RENDERS FIRST AID IN M.I.
PILE-UP
*After what surely must have been a miraculous escape, Sister Netta Rowlands went gallantly to the assistance of the injured in yesterday's pile-up in the mist, the worst since . . .*

Netta put the paper down. How on earth had they got hold of her photograph? She had told the police sergeant her name because he asked for it, but she had not spoken to any reporters. She hadn't even known whether there were any there or not. She picked up the paper again and turned over the page. It couldn't be helped, she supposed. The papers were always after some new slant on the news, and it would all be forgotten in a few days' time. Forgotten far too soon, as far as the accident and its causes were concerned.

Unusually for Netta, though perhaps not surprisingly, she drifted off to sleep again when she had finished her tea and read some of the rest of the paper. By the time she had come to again, had a bath and dressed it was lunch time. She was about to prepare something light when Jerry rang up and informed her that he was bringing in a ready-cooked chicken so as to have lunch with her.

"That O.K. with you?"

"Oh, Jerry, yes, bless you. It will be like old times."

She opened a tin of soup and prepared some vegetables, then put them on to cook. She was setting the table when Jerry arrived, bringing a bouquet of the most beautiful chrysanthemums as well as the chicken and a bottle of wine. He thrust the flowers into her hands.

"From me to you, with love."

She sniffed their woody fragrance, then looked at him, laughing.

"Good heavens, Jerry, I'm not ill. Why all this?"

He grinned. "Let's say they're for the heroine of the hour. Your name was mentioned on the television news last night, did you know?"

She looked at him, startled. "Good lord, all this fuss! Dozens and dozens of people would have done the same in my place. It was nothing. But have you seen the papers this morning? My photograph and everything. How on earth did they get hold of that, I wonder?"

He put the chicken on the table, then thrust his hands in his pockets.

"I'll tell you, if you'll promise not to blow your top."

"It wasn't you? Well, of all the—— But when?"

"Last night while you were out. Elva answered the doorbell and two reporters stood there. Elva thought she'd better bring them up, and they went on their knees almost for a photograph. They asked me how you'd managed to avoid being actually one of the casualties. I told them what you'd told me. I wouldn't be surprised if all kinds of other people want to interview you."

"But this is rediculous!"

"Not so ridiculous. Either your escape was a miracle, or you're a darned good driver. But even good drivers don't always escape. In fact, the one who causes the accident often gets off scot free while the good driver is killed."

"I agree, but in my case it was neither a miracle nor exceptionally good driving. Just common or garden ordinary care."

"But you kept your head, Netta, as well as driving according to the book, *and* you took evasive action. To have done all those things at the same time in those circumstances was a miracle in itself," he insisted.

"In that case it's a pity there aren't more miracles."

"Exactly. And that's what you might be able to get across through some reporters. Now, what about this lunch? I'm starving."

He opened the bottle of wine, and Netta served the first course. It was a happy meal. Again, she felt there was something different about Jerry, and she recalled what he said on the way home yesterday, when she had told him she had missed him. We must talk soon, he had said. Was he by any chance going to ask her to marry him again? If he did, how could she say no? She was fonder of him than she had ever been. They would make each other happy, she was sure. And married to Jerry, she would soon recover from what she felt for Roger, particularly as he was soon to be married. You couldn't nurse a broken heart for ever.

After lunch, Jerry insisted on helping with the washing up, then he took her by the hand and seated her on the small settee, and settled himself beside her, his arm resting on her shoulder.

"There's something I want to tell you, Netta," he said. "But first, I want to know how you feel about one or two things. For instance——" and now his voice became serious. "When we were in the car yesterday, what did you mean by saying you'd missed me and so on?"

She scarcely knew what to say. "Well, I—I meant just that, Jerry."

"No more?"

"I—don't know quite what you mean by 'no more'. I have missed you, Jerry. I've missed you a lot. And I meant it when I said there was nobody I'd rather have seen than you."

His arm tightened across her shoulders. "That can mean anything or nothing, Netta. Let me put it more plainly. Does it mean that you're in any way in love with me—enough, for instance, to marry me?"

## CHAPTER TEN

NETTA caught her breath. The possibility had occurred to her, but she hadn't seriously thought he would ask her. She cast her gaze down for a moment, then looked at him. But he spoke again before she had time to say anything.

"Don't worry, Netta," he said, removing his arm from her shoulders and taking both her hands. "I just thought we ought to get things straight, that's all. I think we both feel the same about each other. Lots of real affection, but in love with someone else."

Her eyes widened. "You mean you—is it Elva?"

He nodded. "Funny, isn't it? I didn't *really* think you'd want to marry me, but it was just that little bit afraid that absence had made your heart much fonder—and I had to know."

She almost laughed. "I'm glad about you and Elva, very. But you would have looked a proper Charley if I'd said yes, I'd marry you, wouldn't you?"

"Ah, ah!" he admonished. "I only asked if you were in love with me enough, that's all. It's a good thing you gave yourself away. If you'd been in love with me, your reaction would have been much quicker—and more joyful. To tell you the truth, Netta, I've only just got things sorted out myself. Yesterday was a bit of a crisis in more ways than one."

"With us, you mean? Yes, I felt it, too. It takes a bit of sorting out at times, this business of one's feelings for someone you've been really close friends with over a long period as we have. You *were* the one person I'd have asked for yesterday, Jerry. I really meant that."

"Because you knew you could cry on my shoulder?" he said, with a grin.

"Something like that. But the emotional state I was in, I could so easily have mistaken it for something else."

"That's what I was afraid of. And at times I wasn't all that sure what it was with me, either.

174

I know now. Fearing you might be lying killed—and it was a very real fear, believe me—I suddenly found the possessiveness had gone out of my feelings for you. Until then, a part of me was always angry with you. Angry because I wanted you in a big way and you didn't want me. Yesterday, you were just a person I had a high regard for, someone I knew well and was desperately anxious about. It was a different kind of love from the other. And as I very much doubt whether it's possible to be in love with a person and *not* be possessive and demanding to some degree, I had to admit that I was no longer in love with you in the way I had been," he gave a sudden grin. "Does any of this make sense to you?"

"Yes, Jerry, it does. It makes a lot of sense," she answered slowly. "You and I can be real friends now. And I'm more glad than I can tell you about you and Elva."

He gave her hands an extra squeeze, then stood up. "Yes—well, I'd like to see you happy, too. But it'll come. Make no mistake." Netta was saved having to make any reply to that by Jerry suddenly remembering something. "By the way, what was all this about you going to London yesterday for an interview for an overseas job?"

"That's right," she said miserably. Then, with something of a shock: "Heavens, that reminds me, I forgot to ring them. What will they think of me?"

Jerry laughed. "I shouldn't worry. They've probably seen the papers and identified you by now. I wouldn't be surprised if they were to ring you. Why do you want to go overseas, anyway? Is it anything to do with Roger Henderson?" She gave a slight lift of her shoulders. "Well, take my tip," he said, "and put the interview off for a while. Things are brewing up here that might surprise you. Will you be in this evening, by the way? It's my half day, Elva's evening. We thought we might come and have a meal with you—and maybe bring somebody to make up a four. Have a little party. But don't you do anything. We'll bring the eats—and drinks. O.K.?"

She said yes, and he made off, saying he had someone to see in town. Netta hoped he wouldn't bring Roger tonight. Or Hugh, either. She couldn't trust herself not to be really rude to him if he started saying things about Roger again.

She felt it was her duty to ring the Nursing Association, not wait for them to ring her. In spite of yesterday's happenings and the newspaper reports, she still owed them an apology for failing to keep her appointment, and in spite of what Jerry had said, she would still go for an interview as soon as it could be arranged. She simply had to get away, make a clean break. It was the only way.

But before she could do so, the doorbell rang, and a woman journalist was on the doorstep, asking Netta for an interview.

"Look" Netta said, "Patiently, this is very good of you, but I've had too much publicity about this already."

"It's very commendable that you should feel that way. But may I please come in and talk to you for a moment and explain what I'd like to do?"

"Very well, Miss——"

"Baxter's the name. And I'm freelance. I'm not on the staff of any paper, though, of course, I contribute regularly."

She was an attractive, friendly person. Netta made some tea, and while they drank it, Miss Baxter explained what she had in mind.

"You may not believe this Miss Rowlands, but some journalists—and I'm one of them—are what you might call idealists. We like to feel that what we're writing is doing some good in the world. So it's not just publicity for you I'm after. In fact, hardly at all, unless you want it—which you don't. No, what I'm interested in is this business of good driving—saving life on our roads. I'm also a feminist. I believe that most of the bad drivers are men. Or let me put it more positively. I believe that women drivers, on the whole, are good. You're one of the ones who has proved it."

Netta laughed. "I wouldn't want to be a party to starting a sex war! And I don't think setting out to prove that women drivers are better than men would achieve anything at all—except a lot of letters to the editor."

"Of course it wouldn't. And I don't intend that. I'm sorry if I've given you the wrong impression. I'm hoping the article will speak for itself, actually, about women drivers. What I'd like from you, Miss Rowlands," the journalist said earnestly, "is your opinion on driving, both from a woman's point of view, and that of a nursing Sister who sees these ghastly sights in the operating theatre. But first, tell me: how long have you been driving a car? As a qualified driver, I mean."

"Not very long," Netta told her. "Three or four months, that's all."

"Well, that would seem to prove that actual experience has very little to do with it. Tell me, what, in your opinion, is the main cause of accidents on the roads today?"

"Human nature," Netta said quickly, recalling with sudden clarity the conversation in the theatre only yesterday, a few hours after the accident. "That was the opinion given by one of our surgeons while actually treating one of the casualties —a child, to be exact—and I agreed with him entirely. So did the other members of the staff who were present."

Miss Baxter wrote swiftly. "Now, that's very interesting indeed. And I'm sure many other people will agree, too. But what kind of faults in human nature, would you say? Aggressiveness, for instance?"

Netta agreed. "And general selfishness. Lack of consideration for the other driver, lack of ordinary courtesy. And above all, perhaps, a diminished, or absent, sense of responsibility. Or perhaps greater still, a refusal on the part of drivers, men or women, to admit that there could possibly be anything wrong with their driving."

"Refusal or reluctance to admit one's mistakes," intoned Miss Baxter. She looked up. "You're right, of course. I'm sure few would deny that. But, you know, you've hit on something very fundamental, really. If human nature itself—character—is to blame. What can be done about it? People say human nature can't be changed. There has to be some other solution. Stronger penalties, things like that."

"You asked me what I thought was the greatest cause," Netta pointed out. "Of course, there have to be penalties, severe ones. But if you say human nature can't be changed and just leave it at that, people won't even *try*, will they? There has to be human endeavor, some effort to change, or improve, otherwise life has no meaning."

Miss Baxter made more notes, and Netta wished she wouldn't. It was hard to remember that this was supposed to be an interview.

"I hope you're not going to quote me *verbatim*. I shall sound an awful prig."

"Don't worry, Miss Rowlands. This is good stuff. Now, tell me about the accident."

"But that's been reported already!" protested Netta.

"Yes, but I'd like to know exactly what your thoughts and reactions were. Please, Miss Rowlands."

And so once more Netta re-lived her experience. After Miss Baxter had gone, other reporters visited her, too, each wanting to write a feature about her. But she declined. She thought the best thing to do would be to absent herself from the flat for a while, so she went for a walk, not staying out too long, in case Elva and Jerry should come, though, of course, Elva had a key.

At about half past six, however, there came a ring at the door, and Netta wondered, as she ran downstairs, whether Elva had forgotten her key or—heaven forbid—whether it was another reporter.

But it was Roger. She stared at him, but he grinned. "Good evening, madam. I'm from the *Daily Spectacular*. Will you grant me an interview for my paper?"

She had to smile. "Goodness, Roger, I've had quite enough of that for one day!"

"May I come in?" he asked. "I want to talk to you. I promise not to mention the M.I."

"I'm sorry." She opened the door wider and asked him in. "Elva and Jerry said something about coming in for dinner," she said, as she led the way upstairs. "I expect there'll be enough to eat for four, if you'd care to stay."

"As a matter of fact, I've just seen Jerry. He told me to tell you they wouldn't be coming in until later, after all."

"Oh?" She invited him to sit down and took a chair opposite him.

Whatever it was he wanted to talk to her about he took his time about beginning. He sat there looking at her, a half smile on his face.

"Can I offer you a drink?" she asked in desperation.

He shook his head. "Not just now, thanks. I thought you might be interested in hearing what I've decided to do. About my writing and everything. To a large extent I'm going to take your advice. But let me take one subject at a time. First, my writing. As I'm still not clear, I've decided to go on as I am for a little while longer, at any rate. I think I shall replace surgery with a writing career some time. But the time is not in the immediate future".

Netta took a deep breath. Why should he want to talk everything over with her? Why not with Iris?

But she answered: "That sounds like a good idea. Often, a certain course *is* right, but because it's not right to do it immediately, we tend to doubt whether it's right at all."

"Exactly. What a clever girl you are!"

She ffushed. "There's no need to be patronizing, Roger," she said stiffly.

His brows lifted. "Patronizing? Whatever gave you that idea? You've got a very clear brain. That's one reason why I——"

He broke off, and Netta guessed what he had been going to say. At least, she thought she had. Now she voiced her previous thought.

"Why you talked this over with me? But shouldn't you be according that privilege to Iris?"

"Ah, yes, Iris," he said, in a matter-of-fact tone of voice. "I'm glad you mentioned Iris. I believe there are some very peculiar rumors going the rounds about Iris and me. Right?"

Netta's heart gave a painful twist. "I thought it was more than rumor. There had been some very strong hints from both of you that you're on the verge of becoming engaged."

"Ah!" he said again, shaking his head. "Hints from Iris and others, perhaps. But not from me. Oh no. As far as I'm corcerned, somebody has been jumping to conclusions. I'll tell you something, Netta, shall I? Those stories, or rumors, or whatever you like to call 'em, were put about deliberately. As a matter of fact, I was told that you were about to become engaged to Hugh Raven."

"What? Good heavens, I've only been out with him about half a dozen times."

"Precisely."

"But—but I don't understand. Who could possibly have told you such a thing about me and Hugh? I'm sure it's not generally rumored, otherwise Elva would have known about it and told me."

"Hugh told me himself."

"But that's perfectly ridiculous!"

Roger grinned widely. "I take it it's not true."

"Of course it's not true!" she caid indignantly. "I don't know what he was thinking about."

"I do. But I'm glad to hear you're not going to marry him, anyway. He isn't really your type. I—er—don't know whether you know of it or not, but Hugh Raven has quite a grudge against me."

"Yes, I know."

Roger eyed her thoughtfully. "Been blackening my character to you, has he?"

"It doesn't matter, Roger. I didn't believe him."

"Not at all?" he queried. "Are you quite sure that he didn't make you doubt me just a little?"

She hesitated. "All right, Roger, if you want the truth. There were times when I did wonder about you."

"In what way? Tell me. I'd really like to know."

But it was difficult. How could she possibly tell him how she had felt that first time he had kissed her? And all the other occasions when he had virtually flirted with her. He had called the rumors about Iris and himself 'peculiar'. But all the same, he had somebody in mind he wanted to marry, obviously.

"The rumors about you and Iris are premature, then?" she asked.

"Premature is hardly the word! I suppose that's why you rushed off when I tried to kiss you the other night, is it? You thought I was a wolf in sheep's clothing, engaged to one woman and trying to make up to another."

"Well, yes—I did think so. Hugh said you— were quite a—sort of lady-killer back at your previous hospital."

"And you believed him?"

"I—didn't want to, but——"

"But what? Go on, this is getting interesting."

"Well, if you must know, Roger, there was that night at the dance when you took me outside and kissed me. Remember?"

Now he was smiling no longer. "I remember all right! But I had reason to think you were behaving badly on that occasion, too. I thought you were Jerry's young lady."

"Then why did you take me outside and kiss me like that?" she retorted warmly.

"Ah, now we're getting down to it, aren't we? It seemed to me that you were positively asking to be taken out and kissed."

Her indignation rose swiftly, but seeing the smile of amusement on his face, and recalling the things she had said to him that night, her anger quickly subsided.

"I was being specially nice to you that evening," she retorted. "I thought you were lonely."

"No—really? That was very sweet of you."

But she colored as she remembered that that night he had come into the dance wearing a dinner jacket, and in the company of Iris, beautifully dressed. Lonely? Hardly.

"Be honest now, Netta. Weren't you just a little bit impish at that dance?"

"Perhaps, but I had been feeling—sort of sorry for you as well. Hugh and Jerry had been saying how much you kept to yourself, and——"

He laughed. "I know. I know all about it." Then all at once he became very serious. He sighed and looked at her. "You know, I really can't keep this up any longer. There's something else I must get straight. Then we can go on talking—I hope. Unless you send me packing."

The way he was looking at her, she thought she must be dreaming. She shook her head in bewilderment.

"What? Saying no to me even before I've said anything?" he said softly. "Netta, come over here and sit beside me. You're too far away over there."

She hesitated. Was this some game he was playing? She couldn't bear it, if it was. She simply couldn't stand being hurt any more. What Hugh had said must be true after all. Roger had a way with women, but he wasn't really serious about any one of them.

"Are you coming?" he asked softly. "Or do you want me to get down on my knees to you? I will if I have to, of course."

"Roger, what *are* you talking about?__ she asked helplessly.

"You don't know? I'm trying to tell you that I'm—in love with you. But you're not giving me much encouragement, are you? If——" He broke off, and Netta's hand flew to her mouth in a gesture of surprise amounting to shock. "Darling," he said then, "come and sit over here beside me."

She rose slowly, as if in a trance, and walked towards him, her heart beating swiftly.

"What are you saying, Roger? You're—not serious, are you? You can't be."

He looked at her in astonishment. "Can't I?" Why not? I've never been more serious in my life. What makes you think I'd joke about a thing like this? You know, you deserve all that's coming to you."

He took hold of both her hands, and as though something withing him suddenly exploded at the contact, he pulled her swiftly down towards him. The next moment she was lying in his arms, and he was kissing her in a way no other man had ever kissed her before. Her joy was so tremendous, all she could do was just cling to him, her heart feeling near to bursting with happiness.

At last he raised his head and looked at her, but he did not let her go.

"Well?" he demanded, his face close to hers. "Do you still think I'm joking?"

She gave a tremulous smile. "You could be. But I adore your sense of humor."

He opened his eyes wide and took a deep breath. "I shall make you suffer for that, you wait and see. Witch! I love you. I'm going to marry you. Is that clearly understood?"

She nodded, blinking away the tears of happiness which threatened to spill over.

"Yes sir, Mr. Henderson, it's understood," she whispered.

He gave her a long look, running his fingers up her cheeks with gentle fingers, then he cupped her face in his hands and covered her lips with his.

"Darling—oh, darling, I adore you. Tell me you love me, Netta, tell me."

She couldn't speak for a moment. She smoothed his hair, giving him kiss for kiss, then unable to keep it back a second longer, she told him what he wanted to hear.

"Oh, Roger, I do love you. I've loved you ever since that night at the dance when you took me outside and kissed me."

"You what?" he exclaimed.

She buried her face in his shoulder, and without looking at him, repeated what she had said.

But he lifted up her face to his. "So! The truth's coming out at last. And do you mean to tell me that you've loved me all this time and I knew nothing about it?"

She grinned. "Not much of a detective, are you?"

"Detective! Heavens, how was I to know?"

"You didn't stop to find out, did you? You kissed me like—like some Don Juan, then left me flat."

"Darling," he said solemnly, "I just couldn't bear it. I was madly in love with you even then. Long before then, as a matter of fact."

"Oh, no!" groaned Netta. "But why didn't you—— Oh, to think of all that waste of time!"

Roger gave a pained grimace. "Darling, don't. It doesn't bear thinking about. As to why I didn't tell you—let's play a game of recap. First, there was Jerry."

"But I was never——"

"I know that now. But I didn't then. Hugh made it his business to tell me."

"But why? Why should Hugh go to the trouble of telling so many lies both to you and to me?"

Roger eased himself into a more comfortable position, resting her head on his shoulder.

"For reasons best known to himself Hugh worked up a positive dislike for me. First he thrust Jerry at me, then when it became known that you two had—sort of split up, he made believe you and he——"

Netta frowned. "Roger, I know all that. At least, I can guess. What I can't understand is—

why was he at such pains to do all this? It seems he left no stone unturned to keep us apart. But why? Surely he didn't know how you felt about me? I certainly never told him how I felt."

Roger gave a grim smile. "I couldn't understand it at first. Then he let it out. In my room, I have a diary. In that diary, your name appears on almost every page. Netta. I'm in love with her. Netta smiled at me today. Today I had a chat with Netta. And so on, and so on. He had gone into my room one day, picked up the diary and read it. Why he should hate me so much, I don't know. But that sort of thing happens sometimes. A person hates you or is jealous of you for no reason at all. Half of it is their imagination. And in most cases, they don't really *do* anything active with their dislike. I'm a writer. I shouldn't say this. But you know, you read in books, seeing plays and films all the things people do to somebody they hate. Like trying to murder them—or actually doing it. Or murdering somebody else and arranging it so that the other one gets the blame. All kinds of things."

"What's known as active dislike."

"Yes, but most times, people content themselves with just telling lies about the one they hate. I suppose there were all kinds of things he could have done to me, things calculated to ruin my career, as they say."

He did quite enough!" Netta said indignantly. "I couldn't make out at the time why he should be saying all the things he did about you. Now, of course, it's only too clear."

"As a matter of interest, what kind of things did he say?" Roger asked carelessly.

She gave a short laugh. "For one thing, he said he had a friend who knew you at your old hospital, and that you were quite a hit with the ladies. He said you had been responsible for breaking up a couple who were engaged, and then you left the girl flat."

"Did you believe him?"

"I couldn't believe you'd deliberately do anyone any harm. I think when he told me that, he must have been getting pretty desperate! Anyway, after that, I decided I'd enough of Hugh, and refused to see him again. I only did in the first place because I felt so wretched on your account."

Roger kissed her. "That man's got plenty to answer for!"

She touched his cheek. "I did think it might have been true that you were a hit with the ladies, though," she told him. "There was that night at the dance, you see."

"That fatal night," he mused. "But you know, before then, you suddenly began being extra nice to me. Why? Could it be that someone had 'sown a tiny seed of love in the garden of your heart'?"

She laughed, enjoying all this retrospect from the safety of his arms.

"That was an old song, wasn't it?" Then, gazing back into the past of a few months ago when she felt so on top of the world, she said thoughtfully: "I must have appeared insufferably bubbly and full of myself about that time."

He smiled, "I remember how full of beans you were. I'll never forget that morning when I was coming out of the theatre and almost collided with you. You looked radiant. Before then, you were just something that nagged at me all the time. But mostly I could forget you when I was writing. Then all at once you were like a bright star——"

"Twinkle, twinkle, little star," she quoted sarcastically. "That was me. Looking back, I don't know how anyone put up with me."

Until then, Jerry had been content with her friendship. She could see that clearly now. Poor Jerry. He had been through a bad time, too.

Roger caressed her hair. "You mustn't talk like that."

"But, Roger, somehow there's something wrong when a person feels like that. It was all froth, not real happiness. There's only a thin dividing line between what is contentment and a proper adjustment to life and what's blindness to people around you. I was too full of self-satisfaction and my own achievements. I was Sister of the new theatre, and I was the proud owner of a car!"

"No mean achievement, surely?" murmured Roger, brushing the smooth curve of her cheek with his lips. "I'd say you had a right to feel pleased with life."

"But not the right to be insensitive to the feelings of other people. Even Elva could see how Jerry felt about me. But I was too blind, too wrapped up in myself to see what was obvious to others."

"But as it turned out, Elva had what you might call a vested interest, hadn't she? She was in love with Jerry herself, and therefore more observant. You couldn't help the way Jerry felt about you."

"I could have saved him from being hurt. And I have a feeling that up to a certain period—when I suddenly felt life was so good—Jerry was no more in love with me than I was with him. It was mainly *because* I was so bubbly and—unwittingly encouraged him that I made him think he was in love with me."

Roger laughed softly. "Darling, few people are as honest with themselves as you are. And I love you for it—if nothing else. I think you're probably right. It's a phase we all go through from time to time. But it's not easy to recognize it for what it is. It's frothy, as you say, for the simple reason that a hundred per cent happiness isn't possible in this world. There's too much suffering all around you. But we *are* allowed a certain amount of happiness you know. Like now, for instance. And like when we're married. Oh, joyful day!"

Netta smiled up at him. "Where shall we live? You must have a study where you can do your writing. And I'll help you, do your secretarial work and so on."

And so punctuated with lovemaking they made plans, talked about life and planned again. And when they got around to thinking about it, they prepared a meal and ate. But inevitably, the time came for them to say good night.

"Elva will be home soon, I'm afraid," sighed Netta.

"I know. This is terrible, having to say good night and leave you. I can hardly bear to wait for the day when I can say good night and stay with you. Darling, we're going to be so happy, you and I. People will point to us and say: now that's what I call an ideal marriage."

She smiled up at him. "So happy. And there's no comparison with the way I feel even now with the way I did when life felt so good."

"Not feeling bubbly?"

She shook her head. "Words can't describe it."

"Try."

"When you're in love you're in tune with the universe," she said slowly. "It's a sort of peace. A feeling of having come into a safe harbor, of coming home after a long and weary journey. Nothing else matters in the world except this time, this place, this moment. There *is* no time. Time has ceased to have any further meaning. There is nothing, at this moment, only you, my darling. Only you—Roger."

Her words served to rob Roger of further speech for a while. He gazed at her in a sort of wonder. Then, swiftly, he gathered her to him once more and kissed her over and over again. Netta felt she had reached the absolute, the ultimate in human happiness.

"Darling, marry me soon. Soon," murmured Roger ardently. "We've wasted so much time, so much time already."

"As soon as you like, my darling. I'm impatient, too," she whispered in reply.

## THE END